Cabin in

Cabin in
By: Shawn R Mosley

www.shawnrmosley.com

Published by
Christine F. Anderson Publishing & Media, Madison VA, 22727
www.publishwithcfa.com

CHRISTINE F. ANDERSON
PUBLISHING & MEDIA

ISBN: 978-0692239612

Printed in the United States of America

Shawn R. Mosley

The Cabin in the Cornfield

By: Shawn R. Mosley

Shawn R. Mosley

Dedication

I would like to dedicate this work to the loving memory of the only father who I have ever known: Moses George, A man who didn't have much but who gave me and my brothers and sisters morals and values in life that can never be erased. You will be deeply missed. Thank you for loving my Momma and staying with her for 35 yrs.

Shawn R. Mosley

Table of Contents

Shawn R. Mosley

Shawn R. Mosley

Author's Note

The characters in this book are fictional, but the message of the book is very prophetic.

There is no separation by color or gender in true Christianity. It is time that the body of Christ becomes one people under the umbrella of love. The purpose of the true gospel message is to help change a life so that life can go on to change another one.

The purpose of the cabin in the middle of the cornfield is to let us know that the people who God wants to use are those who are unrecognized by men on a large scale. Even today God is raising up people from behind the scenes and from obscure places. He is preparing them for his end-time harvest. In this final harvest, all racism in the body of Christ must be destroyed.

My suggestion for those people who are uncomfortable with other races of people is to pray until you get over those issues.

If we really are going to make a difference in this last hour, Christians must love all people no matter what religion, race, or lifestyle they choose. We must be able to love them onto the right path.

Shawn R. Mosley

Chapter 1

Looking Back Over the Years

The bitter wind whistled through the trees in the autumn of a mid-October evening as Jonathan David drove through the quiet streets of Muskegon, Michigan. He was simply amazed as to where his life had ended up. He began to reflect back on the rocky path that he had taken to get to where he was now.

"Let the people say amen! Say amen again! 'Cause the Lord don't make no mistakes. When you belong to God, no matter what you go through, His ultimate plan is to always get you back home in his loving and saving grace. Can I get a witness? I wish somebody else came to have some church this Sunday morning-"

As he continued his drive he smiled as he remembered the eloquent words of the great Reverend P.H. Jackson. His memory served him well; he had only been nine years old when he heard the great pastor. First Missionary Baptist Church; what wonderful memories he had of that church. He thought to himself, *Back then life was so easy, innocent, and promising. All a kid had to do was get into mischief and look forward to Christmas once a year.* He really felt good about finally having a place of rest and contentment in his life. It had all been achieved through a strange but wonderful phenomenon that took place in an old cabin in the middle of a cornfield, in the small town of Medulla, Florida. As a matter of fact many wonderful things happened as a result of that cabin.

1

Shawn R. Mosley

Chapter 2

The Court Room

"Listen young man, you have stood before me over and over again. The last time you were in my court room I promised you that if you were to come before me again that I would sentence you to the Department of Corrections. So now I sentence you to one year and a day in Florida Department of Corrections."

BAM! BAM! The gavel slammed down twice. "Step this way," the bailiff said and motioned for the young man to follow him. Young Jonathan David was escorted off by the very large bald black deputy, who was wearing the usual sheriff's uniform with a black stripe going down the leg. Just looking in his eyes one could easily tell that he took his job very seriously. When it came down locking people up it was just business as usual for him. There was no expression on the man's face; he just pointed his long chubby finger toward the court room exit and nodded his head toward Jonathan. *"That old big foot house nigger; I wonder how it feels to be them white boy's flunky,"* Johnathan thought through the anger and bitterness that had been brewing in his heart since the murder of Erma, his beloved sister.

Dear sweet innocent Erma. His mind reflected back to the time he and Erma had taken the shortcut to school behind the big white church in the boondocks of the country town of Medulla, Florida. "Come on girl, let's get a move on." He said as he looked back at his little sister, who was walking along and dragging her feet.

"I want to wait for Donna." Erma complained as she stood stalling by the fence.

"Girl you had better come on. Mama said that she wanted us to walk together." Jonathan had protested.

"Please my big strong handsome brother, with honey on top of it." She pleaded.

At that point the slam of a truck door caught Jonathan's attention. Through the trees he saw a '57 Chevy white pickup truck with two scuffed up looking older white men standing beside it. Just as he started to say 'no' to her, Donna came running up the pathway with her brother Earlyman walking like he was true to his name. Erma took off to meet Donna mid way down the path. "Hey girl, get back here," Jonathan had called out to his little sister.

"Hey man it's cool--let them walk together; it won't hurt none. You know how Donna and Erma behave when they get together," Earlyman shouted up the path to Jonathan.

"It's more like how they *mis*behave is what concerns me." Jonathan replied back to his friend.

"Aw man, leave 'em be; they'll be just fine." Earlyman continued putting his southern grammar to work.

"Negro, you trippin'. If momma was to find out about this then I would have to move in with You and Mrs. Pearl because I won't be able to go back home. She ain't supposed to be walking by herself. Can you dig it Dude?" Jonathan asked in a stern tone of voice.

"Yeah man, I dig. But she ain't walking by herself! She walking with Donna, also known as "the mouth of the south." She is known to tell everything, so you don't got to worry: if anything goes wrong, my little sister will blab about it. Trust me dude, Donna has got Erma's back. We could use it as leverage for a future bribe to keep them from snitching on us. Anyways, you and me have much more important things to talk about my dear brotha." Earlyman continued.

"Like what?" Jonathan had asked.

"Like the prettiest and finest girl in the school and the whole wide world, none other than Pam Grey."

"Now I *know* you trippin' on something," Jonathan said while looking back at the girls. He remembered noticing that they had picked flowers and put them in each other's hair. He turned back and yelled out to them. "Ya'll better quit playing around and get to school."

"Okay we will meet you there." They said to let him know that they had heard him.

"Don't just meet me there, beat me there. Ya'll got fifteen minutes," he said. She had just looked back at him and smiled. Erma had the kind of smile that always stole her big brother's heart. She was so pure, innocent and warm hearted.

All of a sudden Jonathan's mind flashed back and he was in the damp, musky holding cell waiting to go back into general population. To see the stone cold look in Jonathan's eyes was like staring into a brick wall; he had taught himself how not to show any expression or emotions at all. He could easily be mistaken as he seemed to be a young man without a human soul. He was a very handsome guy who stood at about six feet one inches tall and had a slim muscular frame. He didn't look to be the threat that he was when he lost his temper. There was a hatred and bitterness that ran deep into his very soul.

Chapter 3

Back in the Cell

"Hey man how did it go in court?" An old bald headed man came limping out of cell block 12 called out.

"It is what it is; you know how these white folk get down. They gave a brotha a year and a day."

"Aww that ain't nothin' but a minute young blood." The old man yelled back; Bodi Brown was an old street hustler who was back from the Florida State Penitentiary. He had been convicted for a double homicide. Rumor had it that Bodi had shot and killed two men down in the Liberty City section of Miami because they had tried to cheat him in a card game. Now he was back on appeal hoping to give back a life sentence after serving twenty five years. Bodi was known to most of the inmates as a jail house lawyer; he had been a student of the law since day one of his conviction. "Listen: the way that you beat up on that other fellow, you are lucky that they didn't try to get you for attempted murder. Whenever a man has did as much time as I have done then you automatically know a stone cold killer when you see one. And you are one. Now don't get me wrong--there's some people who only talk the talk but they won't bust a grape in a fruit fight, know what I mean? But when I look at you, I see a dangerous man. You kind of remind me of myself and how I use to be." He paused but he was not finished. "You are just too bitter and evil. If you don't change your ways, you're going to end up just like me--fighting for your very own freedom. Now you can take an old fool's wise advice." He said with a crooked smile. Old man Brown got up from the day room and limped back into his cell. *These young boys don't know what they are getting themselves into.*

Jonathan could still hear the old man talking from inside the cell. "It seems like everybody has all the answers nowadays. He needs to worry about getting his old antique self out of prison. That's what he should be worrying about. And stop getting in my business. It ain't gonna cost him a dime to stay the heck up out of mine." Jonathan smarted off with his southern slang. But in his heart he knew that the old man was right about what he was saying. In his mind he just wasn't ready for a change. *Human life means absolutely nothing to me. My own life don't even matter, so why in the world would I care about anyone else? It's not going to happen. I have failed at everything in life because I am a failure. I receive my fate. And since I am forced to live this type of life I am going to live it to the fullest of my ability. There is no love in this black man's heart for these racist white people and their*

5

system. For a black man there is no justice but just-us. We have to get it how we live. These corrupt thoughts constantly ran through his mind. His perspective was the only way that he was trying to see life. *Yeah, Bodi is a good old dude but he just don't understand,* Jonathan thought as he sat on his bunk.

Chapter 4

Off to Prison

"Frank Thorton, Robin Engram, Derrick Mosley, Toney Flinoy, pack your bags! We will be back in ten minutes to get you." Jonathan could hear the jailer calling the inmates in dorm two. *Man I sure do hope that they call my name out tonight. I am ready to ride and get this time started so that I can get back to the streets.*, he thought to himself. *I'll just go up there and do this little bit of time and come back home harder than I was before*, he continued in thought. The big fat jailer came down the hall dangling his keys. Jonathan sat straight up on his bunk. "Alright dorm one: when I call out your names, pack your bags and roll up your mattresses and wait at the sliding door. James Booker, Mitch Flowers, Steven Washington, Jonathan David, and Kenny Brooks. Pack your bags I'll be back to get you in fifteen minutes."

Eighty men were shackled together from the waist with hand and foot irons connected. They made their way to the Blue Bird bus that was heading to Lake Butler R.M.C. The drive was long and tedious; the men road silently down the highways heading northward until the silence was finally broken from the back of the bus. "Hey John--how much time did you end up with?" A tall big muscular brother called up front to Jonathan.

"Oh they just gave me one and one." He answered.

"Yeah you'll be finish with that in no time." The man yelled back.

"What about you?" Jonathan asked.

"They gave me five and a half with twelve months county time credit. I figure I'll end up pulling eighty percent of three and a half years. Considering that I had two robberies and a kidnaping charges I didn't do too bad." He said. The men went back to total silence as they continued on their journey not fully knowing what was in store for them up ahead. Jonathan closed his eyes and the nightmare vision, as he liked to call it, started all over again.

"Hey Jonathan, did you see Donna? She was supposed to be waiting over by the bench for me." Earlyman asked.

"No man I haven't seen Erma either. Maybe they are still talking to Mrs. Brooks. Let's go to her class and see if they are there." Jonathan said.

"Okay let's do it," answered his best friend and home boy. They walked around to the classroom and peeked into the window of the door. It was completely empty. Frantically they both looked at each other and ran to the parking lot "Hey there go Mrs.Brooks right over there!" Earlyman said. They both ran over to her.

"Hey Mrs. Brooks!" They both cried out trying desperately to get her attention. She made a pause and turned around to see who it was that was calling her. She looked up and saw Jonathan and Earlyman coming quickly toward her.

"Hello boys; how can I help you?" She asked.

"We can't seem to find our sisters. Do you know if they have already left or not?" asked Jonathan.

"No! They wasn't in school today. I was going to ask you guys what happened and why they were not in class," she responded.

"No they wasn't in school today...No they wasn't in school today...No they wasn't in school today..."

Mrs.Brooks' words played in Jonathan's head over and over like a broken record. He snapped out of the nightmare vision and found himself back on the prison bus. The many sleepless nights of tormenting troubles and pain had been the result of his reflections on the past through those visions. It made the horrible event that took place so long ago seem as if it was just yesterday.

Chapter 5

Violence on the Yard

Beep! Beep! Beep! Beep!

Awakened by the sound of the noisy siren and bull horn, Jonathan sat up on his bunk.

"*Please get back to your pods now! If you do not get back to your housing units then you will cause us to have to use excessive force this is a verbal warning.*" The correctional officers in the gun towers were all staring down into the prison yard. Tom Cat from Miami had been killed in a brutal stabbing by Lil Fila; word was that Tom Cat had been intercepting Lil Fila's mail and writing love letters to his woman. Since Fila was from Jacksonville, there was expectation that the Miami crew was going to retaliate but no one knew when or how. The Miami boys had caught the Jacksonville boys in the day room while they were watching the football game; Miami rushed into the room with shanks drawn and began to stab them to death.

Jonathan looked out of his cell window, scanned the yard, and saw what looked like a battle field of gladiators going to war. Instantly his blood began to boil with adrenalin. The inmates were running across the yard with shanks the size of swords and ran each other through with them. Some other inmates were shooting each other with Zip guns, or as some called them, toothpaste guns. *I have got to get in on this*, Jonathan thought to himself. He quickly reached into his mattress through a small hole and grabbed a sharp piece of metal that had an electrical taped handle on one end. He rushed out to the yard and got right smack dab in the heat of the battle, which was intense; there was shedding of much blood, sweat and tears. Although he wasn't from Jacksonville or Miami, the thrill of violence burned through his veins. The pain that he lived with in his heart every day had to be released upon something or someone. He crouched down at the corner of the gym and saw two of the men from Jacksonville coming toward his direction. *I'll stick both of these dudes and then I will move around to the other side before anyone notices what I have done*, he thought to himself. Just as the two young men neared the corner of the gym, Jonathan felt a sharp pain shoot through his shoulders and upper back. He looked back over his left shoulder and saw the butt of a shank sticking out of his flesh. He reached and pulled the knife-like object out of his burning flesh and turned toward his attackers to counter the attack. He looked into the face of murderous anger. There was a big

9

black brother staring him right in the eyes with a mouth full of gold teeth. All of a sudden fear began to grip Jonathan's heart because his eyes were getting blurry and his vision was fading in and out. "That's right fool: die," the man said as he noticed the effect that the stab wound was having on Jonathan.

"He's out of there." One of the other two men said as they both took off in the other direction. As he faded in and out, Jonathan realized he was lying on the ground. *Am I dead?* He asked himself. He noticed the taste of blood in his mouth and slowly lifted up his head. He then realized that he was now laying in a puddle of his own blood. His head began to spin as he dropped his head down to the cold concrete floor and blacked out.

Chapter 6

The Other Side

I can see myself laying there on the ground. Jonathan thought to himself as he looked down upon his own body. The paramedics were working frantically on the now still and lifeless figure that looked very much like Jonathan. *But how can this be?* "Hey! I am right here. I am right here!" He repeated over and over. But nobody seemed to be able to hear him. All of a sudden in the flash of a split second he was traveling through what seemed like a tunnel of wind. He wanted to stop but he had no power to do so. All he knew at that moment was that he was moving very fast through what felt like a windy tunnel. Almost instantly he found himself standing outside the gates of the most beautiful place that he had ever seen or could imagine. The beauty in the colors there were magnified a thousand times beyond those that were back in the world he had known. He looked up at the massive gate that seemed to have no end and reached beyond a most beautiful sky. Jonathan was in awe when he realized that the gate in front of him was really a gigantic pearl. Inside the gate there appeared to be a majestic city that had no end to it. Running through the mist of the city was what seemed to be a river. But it wasn't just any river: this one appeared to be made out of pure crystal water. In the middle of the gate there was a sign that had an inscription that caught his attention that read

{HAR-TSIYYOWN}

Before he could ask himself what was its meaning, the answer came seemingly out of nowhere: Mount Zion the city of God. It was as if nothing was hidden or covered up in this place. He looked inside the gate and noticed that there were people walking everywhere throughout that wonderful city. Their eyes seemed to have so much joy and peace, the kind he had never known. At that very moment in his heart there was nothing he wanted more than to be inside of that gate with all of those happy people! He ran up to the gate and began to shake and pull on it but it didn't move.

His haste caused him to overlook the tall giant who held a big book in his hands. "For you no reservations have been made as yet." These words came from this man who appeared to be about eleven feet tall and he spoke without opening his mouth. Then all of a sudden a radiantly beautiful black girl who appeared to be about nineteen years old came close to the gate. This young lady appeared to be someone

11

who had an instant connection with him. His heart was instantly drawn to her. She also began to communicate without ever saying a word from her lips. However the voice was very audible and every word was clearly perceived by him.

"Jonathan it is so good to see you, and I look forward to seeing you again one day but you can't come in as of now until it is made right. That which you think is really just what you think," she said. "Look upon the radiance of the light that is upon the throne."

At that very moment a throne full of light came out of the heart of the beautiful city and no one could stand upon their feet. The throne was brighter than the sun and energy; Jonathan felt strength passing through his body as he fell under its power. Each wave of light filled him with contentment. In the shift of his eyes he was laying on a gurney looking up at the surgical lights now above him. "Wow, I am sure glad to see your eyes open up. For a moment I thought that we lost you. We had to work extra hard to stop the internal bleeding. Fortunately for you we did. Miracles indeed still happen today," The doctor said and walked out of the room. Jonathan looked around the room and noticed that there was a prison guard sitting over in the corner. After his experience it really didn't even matter to him that he was in the prison infirmary. There was such a strong sense of peace and tranquility in Jonathan that he knew somehow he had been given another chance. He stayed in the infirmary for the remainder of his prison stay. With his six months county jail time all that was required for him to finish his sentence was six more months and a day which went by fast. He was haunted by the nightmare visions and the bitter racism of his past but he was about to experience something that went beyond all human logic. Out of all the things that was revealed at the beautiful gate, he was constantly puzzled by questions in his mind: Who was that young beautiful girl who seemed to personally know him? What did the girl mean when she said, *What you think is just what you think*? And what did he have to make right before he entered into the gate? None of these things made sense to him at all but he pondered them in his mind from time to time while he waited for his sentence to finish.

Chapter 7

The Cabin

June 21st was the day that it all began.

As Jonathan walked down the dusty old dirt road, a pickup truck drove past him doing about 90 miles an hour. If he had not moved a little to the right of the road the truck would have dragged him clear down to Mr. James' house at the end.

"Hey haven't you yet learned to stay out of the middle of the darned road?" The driver yelled back as he sped off into the distance.

Jonathan became furious, reached down, picked up a rock from the ground, and threw it after the truck but missed it by a mile. "Stupid jerks, those people think they own the world. Now they want the roads. White people: go figure." He said out loud in anger. As he continued to walk, he noticed a pathway leading off the dirt road into the cornfield. He never noticed this road before. Out of pure curiosity he decided to venture off down the pathway and investigate. As he walked deeper down into the cornfield he saw a wooded area and an old run down cabin.

There it was, sitting right in the middle of the massive stalks of corn. Outside of the cabin was that same blue dodge pickup truck that almost run him over. *I've got a bone to pick with this dude. I knew that there was a good reason for me to walk down through this field. Now I am gonna give him a piece of my mind*, he thought as he clenched his fist tightly and stormed toward the cabin. On the left side of the cabin was a pigeon coop. As he glanced down at the ground he saw feathers and blood leading up to the front porch. Just as he went to knock on the door, Jonathan looked through the window at the top of it. He saw the driver of the truck; he was a tall lanky white fellow and was standing there polishing down a 12 gauge shot gun. In the corner of the room was an overweight woman sitting with a steak knife and eating corn on the cob. Jonathan raised his hand to knock, but looking at the tall man sitting there with that shot gun caused him to have second thoughts. Instead he decided to just put his ear to the door. "I really do hate those blacks sneaking around here," the man said.

"Now Billy Ray, why in the name of God would you say a thing like that?" The lady asked.

"Well just look at it, Suzy Ann; they creep around here and take what don't belong to them whenever they feel like it. I tell you what, the

13

next time I see one on this property I am going to blast it to kingdom come. They remind me of those tree coons back home in Mississippi. I killed my fair share of them from a distance. Yeah, they tried to run but I put the dogs on them. They squirmed around on the ground until I walked over to them and bang! Lights out!" He said it with a smirky grin on his face as he sat back in his chair.

"Billy Ray Parker you ain't changed a bit." The fat lady said.

"Nope and don't plan to." He replied.

Jonathan stood outside the door in shock. *I can't believe what I just heard. These crazy white folk is killing off black people*, he thought to himself. He waited for a few more minutes to listen to be sure that he had heard correctly.

"Well Billy Ray, you can call them boys and make sure that they come by and pick up them white sheets that I made for them because they gonna need them tonight." Suzy Ann said.

Man I can't take this no more; I have got to do something about this. If I don't then this crazy white Ku Klux Klan bunch is going to kill a lot of innocent people. Jonathan thought as he bolted off the front porch and ran as fast as he could back through that cornfield. He didn't stop until he was back on that old dusty dirt road. Jonathan walked about a mile down the road before he stopped and sat under a tall pine tree on a milk crate.

"Listen boys, tell me where did you last see your little sisters?" The detective asked.

"Well sir, we left them on the path behind the church." Earlyman answered.

"And what church are you referring to?" The detective asked.

"The one that Reverend Bradley preaches at," Jonathan said.

Mrs.Brooks intervened for the boys. She could tell they were having a hard time answering some of the detective's questions. "It's the church over by the wooded area about a half mile down the road. The name of the church is Bethel Missionary Baptist Church."

"Did you see anybody standing around that area this morning that you weren't used to seeing? Like any strange faces that you have never saw before?" The detective asked.

"No, sir!" Both of the boys said at the same time.

"Oh wait," said Jonathan. "I do remember looking through the trees and seeing those old white men standing by a pickup truck; it looked kinda like my Uncle Monroe's truck. But it was white and Uncle Monroe's truck is green."

"Do you know what kinda truck your Uncle Monroe has, son?" The detective continued to ask.

"Yes sir it's a Chevy."

"Man, what you doing sitting out here by this tree, daydreaming?" Jonathan looked up to see who had asked him the question. It was Earlyman. He was a jet black brother with a muscular frame. He stood about six feet four with a head full of brush waves in his hair.

"Hey what's up, my dude?" The sound of Earlyman's voice brought Jonathan back to reality.

"You still having all those weird daydreams?" Earlyman asked his best friend.

"Yeah after a while you just kind of learn to live with it. But we have a much bigger problem than that," Jonathan answered. "Man, wait until you hear what I just witnessed go down: Some of these white folks got a plan for us blacks around here. And we've got to be ready for whatever comes our way."

"Hey, slow down, low down. I can't feel ya 'cause you're talking too fast. So break it down in a way that I can dig it," his boyhood partner contested.

"Yeah it all started when I was walking down that dirt road on my way home and suddenly this old ugly truck drove past me so fast that it almost ran me off the road. As far as I was concerned the driver was just one of those kind that scream obscene slurs out of the window and keep on moving and you hope you never see them again. You know those kind?" Earlyman nodded and he continued. "So I picked up a rock from the ground and threw it and almost knocked out his back window," he lied. "So then this lanky red neck backed up his truck and yelled out of the window and that's when all the racial slurs started. At this point I was fed up so I rushed towards the truck and he took off." Jonathan lied again. "I just continued to walk and then I noticed a path that went down through the cornfield. Believe it or not something on the inside of me started tugging at my heart telling me to check it out and find out where it led. So I did. Right smack dab in the middle of that cornfield there it was an old wooden cabin. And check this out: Next to it was that same pickup truck that almost ran me off the road. That's when I walked up on the porch and started to knock on the door and put that old hillbilly in his place. The only reason that I didn't is because he was holding a twelve gage shot gun and his fat old lady was sitting there waving a buck knife with a long shiny blade. I wasn't afraid of them, I am just not stupid. They are the kind of people who will kill first and ask questions later," Jonathan explained.

"That has got to be the worst story that I have ever heard. Just because a racist white man has a shot gun and his wife has a knife doesn't make them killers. You was born and raised here in Medulla. You are not new to prejudiced people," Earlyman said.

"Yeah I know but that's not all the story" Jonathan interrupted. "Now get this," he continued. "I heard them talking about them getting their sheets and killing black people like tree coons."

"What in the world is a tree coon?" Earlyman asked.

"You know, trees were they hung coons. Isn't that what they used to call black people? Niggers and coons? Hello! Earth to Earlyman! Is there anybody home? I need you to pay attention!" Jonathan said.

"It is 1987, not 1947; that kind of stuff don't fly today. I really think that you are worrying about nothing."

"Trust me man, it's something." Jonathan continued to engage in conversation with his buddy and friend throughout the evening trying to convince him to help stop what he perceived was going to happen.

Chapter 8

Back at the Cabin

"Suzy Ann, do you know that them cats got into my pigeon coop again? I found two more dead this morning. Those wild big black tom cats sure remind me of those raccoons and how they hide up in the trees and wait for a proper time to come down and steal off our property. They sneak through the fence and steal all of our birds. I hate those blacks because they are the meanest of all the cats that I have ever saw." Billy Ray poured out his thoughts to his wife.

"Well Billy Ray, one thing for sure you just can't go around shooting domesticated animals just because they been feeding on those birds of yours. They are liable to call the humane society on ya." Suzy Ann replied.

"Hey did that sweet old lady down on the canal send her grandsons over to pick up them sheets that I made for their beds?" She asked.

"Yeah they came around 5 in the P.M." Billy Ray answered. "You know Suzy Ann, I really do feel bad about the fact that I almost run over that black feller who was walking on the dirt road. I was just in such a big hurry to make it home to you so that I could give you that insulin shot. The last time your sugar went so high, you almost went into a diabetic coma. It scared me half to death. But I still should have been a little nicer to that feller. I think as the Godly man that I am the next time I see him I owe him an apology."

"Well Billy Ray, don't fret none; you are bound to see him again and I know that you will do the right thing." She responded back. "Let's join hands and pray for that young man. Maybe God will touch his heart."

Right there in that old wooden cabin Billy Ray and his wife began to pray for the Lord's will to be done in Jonathan's life. And those prayers were about to cause a lot of strange events to take place before they were made a reality.

17

Shawn R. Mosley

Chapter 9

New Neighbors

The vacant sign was being removed from the edge of the lawn. An old funny looking man with a slightly humped back and a bald spot in the top of his egg-shaped head who was wearing a pair of bifocal glasses and a too small suit was removing it. A two-ton U-Haul truck sat in the drive way of the ranch style brick home. A few men carried the furniture into the house. Suddenly a burgundy Fleetwood Cadillac pulled up with two passengers in the front seat. It appeared to be two women but from where Jonathan and Earlyman stood it was hard to tell; for some reason on that day the sun was shining brighter than usual. "I believe there is two girls in that car right there." Earlyman said.

"You say that about every car," Jonathan replied.

"How much do you want to bet?" His friend cried out.

"I ain't going to bet you nothing." Jonathan said.

"Well, let's just see." Earlyman said, standing there with his arms folded. Finally an older brown complexioned woman who looked to be in her early fifties or late forties got out of the driver's side. For an older woman she was very shapely and well put together. In other words, the woman was fine. The second female to exit the car was younger, maybe half the age of the first one. When the young men caught a glimpse of her it seemed as if time just stood still.

"Man, she is absolutely borgeous." Jonathan said. That was his combination word; it was short for "beautiful" and "gorgeous." She stood about five feet and had a beautiful caramel complexion. She had curves from shoulders to toes on a petite frame with nothing missing, nothing to be desired, and nothing broken. She was all together. When she stepped out of the car, it seemed like her movements were in slow motion. The wind caught her silky black hair and caused a teasing effect.

"Like mother like daughter. If the saying is true that 'you are what you eat,' then they must be eating fine food from a fine food restaurant because they are so fine." Earlyman said.

"You can slap me five on that." Jonathan said as he gave his friend some dap. The two young men stood around and admired the beauty of the two ladies until they finally got back into their burgundy Cadillac and drove off.

Jonathan continued to talk over with Earlyman day in and day out about his encounter at the cabin. There was two things that were the bulk of their conversations: The beautiful new girl and those country hicks living in the middle of the cornfield. Jonathan was determined that he was going to investigate both of them further. He knew that one was for his pleasure and the other would be for those hillbillies' pain. In Jonathan's mind all white people were bad, especially since Erma's death. In a situation like the one that he felt that he was now facing, where he felt they were planning to hurt a bunch of black people, was right up his alley. He welcomed this type of war with open arms. Now if he could just get his old buddy Earlyman to get on board with him, then the battle would be on.

Chapter 10

I Got To Have That Girl

8 A.M. Saturday morning, and the tall oak trees were swaying in the wind. The sound of mocking birds were singing to welcome the bright morning sun. Mr. Miller and Mr. James were cutting their lawns on riding lawn mowers. Things in the small country town of Medulla couldn't get much better. Or could they? Just as Jonathan opened the window of his bedroom to take in the awesome morning scene, he looked down and saw the new girl whom he had it bad for. "It sure is a beautiful day in the neighborhood. Would you be my neighbor?" He said, mocking Mr.Rogers. He had learned that her name was Brenda Jackson. She had moved to Medulla from Muskegon, Michigan with her mother, Trudy Jackson. Rumor had it that Trudy was married to a professional football player who she later divorced and sued for a lot of money. She was a certified gold digger. When it came to men she changed them like she changed her underwear. Men were only one thing to Trudy: A source for more material things. If a man couldn't buy her all the things that she wanted then plain and simple, she had no need for them. As he made his way outside, Jonathan wondered if Brenda was that way also. "Hello, beautiful how are you? So sweetie, do you have a name?" Jonathan said, acting as if he didn't already know her name. He continued to flirt but she paid him no mind as she washed the parked car. "So, how about dinner sometime; can I take you out for a bite to eat? So, what do you like to do for fun?" He continued to talk but she gave him no answer. "Anyways, it's good to meet you." He said as he backed away; he did not notice the sprinkler sticking up out of the ground and as his foot hit it he lost his balance and fell over it. Brenda burst out laughing. Jonathan sat there for a few minutes then he broke out in a hysterical laugh too. "Now you have to go out with me because you're the first woman that I ever literally fell for."

She turned and gave him the warmest smile and said, "Nope."

"Listen pretty lady, I have already fallen for you so what else can a brother do to show you that I am interested in you?"

"Mmmm let me see," she said. "Can you come and approach me like the lady that I am and not use that same old line that I hear every day?" She took her hand and grabbed her crotch as if she were a guy and began to mock Jonathan: "'*Hello, beautiful. Baby, you know you fine. Would you be mine, all mine?*' Now do you see how lame that

21

sounds? Why don't you try using a more natural approach and just try being yourself. Dare to be different. I want an original not a copy."

Jonathan stood up, took her by the hand, and while looking her straight in her eyes he said, "Brenda, I really do think that you are a pretty girl and I would consider myself honored above men if you would go out with me."

"Well that's a little better, Mr. Clumsy-can't-stand-on-your-own-two-feet. Let me think about it and I will tell you later when you call me." She reached into the passenger side of the car, took out an ink pen and wrote her phone number in the palm of his hand. Call me around five tonight."

"Yeah I will holler--" he caught himself and changed his tone. "I mean, I'll give you a call around that time."

Just as Jonathan started out of Brenda's driveway, he saw the blue pickup truck speed off down the street and Billy Ray Parker was driving. *Somebody need to stop this dude, and that somebody is going to be me*, he said to himself. The experience that Jonathan had while he was at the beautiful gates caused him to somewhat slowdown from a lot of his previous behavior that drove him but there still remained a mean streak in him against all white people for what a few had done to his little sister Erma. He wasn't going to be at peace until he hurt someone the same way he was hurting. He wanted someone else to grieve and feel the pain that he felt when his only sister was taken out of his life. He was going to prove the saying true, that hurt people will hurt people.

The deep hatred and racism that was in Jonathan's heart was enough to trigger those nightmares at the very sight of Billy Ray. "Oh my God; Sheriff, I can see a few drops of blood that is leading behind the church." One of the sheriff's deputies had reported back to his commanding officer. The constant barking of the bloodhounds could be heard from the wooded areas as the search had continued for the missing girls. The dogs pulled vigorously through the brush. The barks got louder and the dogs more determined as they got closer to their intended goal. Jonathan stood close to his mom who was holding his hand behind the church as they had watched more deputies enter the woods with flashlights and shotguns. "Oh my sir; I think you better come and take a look at this. Uggh uggh!" The sound of the deputy gagging and vomiting came over the walkie-talkie. "Oh my God--I have never saw anything like this before," the deputy continued. Jonathan had overheard the deputy and had snatched away from his mom to head for the woods.

"Hey John, you got me man?" Earlyman's voice brought Jonathan out of the daydream.

The haze and fog cleared Jonathan's mind. "Oh, my bad bro. I guess I was kind of caught up for a moment." Jonathan replied.

So you still having those terrible visions huh?" Earlyman asked.

"Yeah man I guess I will have them for the rest of my life. It's strange how Erma and Donna has been gone for ten years and I still can't seem to get the vivid memories out of my head. It's like something inside of me is still holding me to that day when it first happened." Jonathan said as he looked off in a state of confusion.

"Bro, that's probably because you are so hard. I remember when we were kids you fell down a flight of stairs and didn't even cry. You just got up, rubbed your head, and kept moving. Remember when your mom used to beat you with that belt and you would just look back at her with that mean look on your face? It was right then and there I knew that we were going to be partners forever. Because everyman need a crazy partner. Negro are you even human?" He said jokingly.

"All right, enough of the dry humor and tell me what it was that you were trying to tell me." Jonathan demanded as he looked his friend right in the eyes.

"I said that I would help you to deal with them racist white people who live in that cornfield. Do you have a plan?"

"Yeah, I got one but it requires that we run in on them with pistols drawn."

"Bro, are you sure of what you heard"? Earlyman asked to make sure.

"Listen man, I have never been surer of nothing in my whole life." He answered.

"Okay then, I am down with you on this but I know how much you don't like white folks so you have got to promise me that nobody is going to get hurt. All we gonna to do is scare them all right?"

"Okay you have a deal." Jonathan agreed.

Shawn R. Mosley

Chapter 11

Life is Good

It was a breezy summer night. Billy Ray and Suzy Ann Parker sat on the porch watching the old pigeon coop to make sure those Tom cats didn't find a way to get in. "You know Suzy Ann, I was wondering if there was anything that I could do to show the love of God to these people in this town."

"Don't worry Billy Ray, you always seem to find a way. That's just the kind of good man God made you to be. Ever since you accepted the Lord into your life you have almost put us in the poor house. Every time I turn around you are buying food for the neighbors and letting complete strangers sleep on our couch. I sure do wish that God would call someone else to give away everything that they own to the poor other than my husband." She said jokingly.

"You know that the black folk on this side of town don't take to kindly to us being around here ever since those two little colored girls got murdered over here by those two white men about ten or eleven years ago, Billy Ray answered.

"Yeah I know honey, but I have never met a person that you couldn't win over. Once they get to know you they will love you. You are just a natural when it comes down to gaining favor with people. Yes I must admit that sometimes I do worry about us. The way that the world is today people are liable to just come up and hurt us for no good reason at all," his wife commented.

"Well sugar plum, don't you worry that sweet little head of yours. The Lord has always protected us. I believe that he has angels watching over us. Nobody can just do whatever they want to a child of God unless He lets it happen. I have always believed that way."

Suzy Ann smiled and as she laid her head on Billy Ray's shoulder, she was comforted in the fact that their life was good and peaceful because they were dedicated to live for God. The Parkers sat there together that day, thankful for life.

Jonathan and Brenda had really grown fond of each other. The flames of romance were kindling between them. It seemed as if they both had so much in common except it didn't matter to her about the color of a person's skin. She was the type of person who was won or

25

lost by other people's personalities. She constantly talked to Jonathan about forgiving the people who took the life of his little sister. Jonathan would quickly change the subject and think to himself, *The poor girl just don't understand.* He viewed the whole white race as people without hearts. In his mind there was a fear of them and his only defense was to face them with hostility and hatred. He taught himself to retaliate in aggression and rage. He couldn't get it to register in his mind how two grown white men could rape and murder two innocent little black girls.

The many terrible stories that Jonathan had heard while growing up in the south had helped to shape his perception as well as fuel the fire of hatred that stemmed from his personal experience. *White people just don't like black people and if they had it their way then they would get rid of us all.* That was Jonathan's view on life and the only thing that could change it was the miracle from God which he would soon get. Then he would learn what the saying truly meant, that all men are created equal.

Brenda would often look at her strong handsome prince and she would feel sorry for him because she knew that unless he changed his attitude about whites then he would never reach his full potential in life. She also knew that type of hatred would steal some of their most precious and intimate moments. *How can I make him see that his point of view is wrong? People are just people and there is good and bad in every race,* she thought to herself.

Yes a change was soon about to come in the small town of Medulla. And although things would get worse before they would become better, change still was on the way.

Chapter 12

A Murder in Medulla

"Oh Lord God, give me the wisdom to hear your voice. Lead me by your precious Holy Spirit. Bless these people here in Medulla." Billy Ray was kneeling down at the foot of his bed praying and crying out to God. Suzy Ann was already snuggled up asleep under the covers. For some strange reason Billy Ray was led to stay up and pray. When he had finished praying he waited to see if God would give him some divine insight.

All of a sudden he heard a loud clear voice that said, "Get your wife and leave out the back door, take her car and go to her sister's house in Lakeland. I have some plans for a few unexpected guests."

Billy Ray walked over to the bed to wake his wife. He stood there looking down upon her for a moment and admired his companion and best friend of 30 years. He knew that she wasn't that skinny young girl that he fell in love with thirty years ago, but his love for her was even stronger now than when they first got married. *What in the world would I do if something ever happened to my beautiful Suzy Ann? Lord thank you for her*, he thought to himself. He woke her up and she looked at the clock on the night stand by the bed.

"Oh honey, it's only 11:35 P.M. Can we just get some sleep and you can tell me what's troubling you in the morning?" Suzy Ann asked.

"No honey; I was in prayer and the Lord told us to leave right now and go to Florence's house." Billy Ray contested.

"All right," she said and they both started getting ready to leave.

The young men's feet made crunching sounds in the dried leaves as they neared the old cabin in the middle of the cornfield. "Hey man can you step a little softer? You are making too much noise." Jonathan said to Earlyman as they crept pass the pigeon coop.

Hissss!!! Reeern!!! Earlyman accidentally stepped on the tail of a black Tom cat and got too close to a second. Both of the young men were caught-off guard by the frightening sound. Earlyman was leading the way, turned to run back, and ran right into Jonathan. They both fell into an old horse water trough and dropped their guns to the ground.

"What you running for, man?" Jonathan whispered. "It's only a black cat. With your big scary self. Now look at what you done, went and got both of us soaked and wet." They both climbed out of the

27

smelly water and felt around on the ground to retrieve their pistols.

"Hey man, I want you to remember that we are only trying to scare these people out of town. I ain't going back to the pen on no murder beef, especially for killing no white folks." Both men reached into their back pockets and pulled out ski masks and put them on to cover their faces.

"Okay I am ready now man." Earlyman said as he stood there, shaking and chilled from the cold water in the trough.

"Boy, you sure is one scary dude man. If I had known that you was this scared then I would have did this by myself," Jonathan said shaking his head in disgust.

"Listen here muh-muh-man, ain't nobody scared. I am just cold from falling in that water over yonder, that's all. S-so you cu-cu-can just lay off me with the nonsense because I will leave you right here." Earlyman was agitated with his partner.

"Don't trip, man; we've got work to do." Jonathan reminded him. With both pistols drawn, they walked up on the porch. "Listen man you check the back door and I will check the front door."

"Hey, brother; what if that crazy old hick go for his gun? Then what should I do?"

"Shoot in the air and hope that he is too scared to make the complete move for it. If that don't work, get low and run like heck. Now go!" Jonathan commanded. Earlyman took off toward the back of the cabin. Jonathan grabbed the front doorknob; he barely turned it and it was open. The cabin was dark and eerie as he stepped over the threshold and into the room. The old wooden floor squeaked at his every step as he tried to tip through. A shadow of light was cast from behind him as the door opened wider at his back. Earlyman had come in through the front door anyway. Both of the young men's hearts were racing; they did not know if something unexpected would soon happen. They moved from the living room into the bedroom on the left. They slowly opened the door and all they saw was a bed that was very neatly made up and a clock on the wall that read 11:35 P.M. "Listen man, we don't have all night." Jonathan whispered. "It's getting late; come on let's hurry up and get this over with." They went into another room and it was filled with boxes, papers, an old safe and a file cabinet, but there was no trace of Billy Ray or Suzy Ann. Finally they got to the last room and there was a crack in the door. A gleam of light glowed out into the hallway. Jonathan could tell that it was from a T.V. set. Both of the young men slowly entered the room.

All of a sudden the room began to spin and both men found

themselves losing consciousness and falling to the floor. The room kept on turning as their vision faded in and out as they looked up at the ceiling. They both lay there helplessly as total darkness closed in on them.

As they regained consciousness, they noticed that the room smelled of fresh gun fire. They looked beside themselves and noticed two bullet casings in the middle of the floor. Suddenly a gush of wind swept through the room along with the sound of what sounded like the wings of a giant bird of some kind. Jonathan looked to the left of the room and saw what looked like a large pair of wings covered in golden glitter vanish through the wall. "Uh man, did you see that?" He asked his friend; Earlyman was shaking his head as if he had been hit from behind and was attempting to regain his composure.

"Man listen, I ain't saw nothing. And I don't believe that I am here with you on this crazy mission of yours. And as soon as I can get to my feet then I am out of here." He said to Jonathan. As Earlyman arose to his feet, his face seemed to go pale and his mouth dropped wide open. "Oh my God! Man you didn't! Please tell me you didn't."

"Man what in the world are you talking about?" Jonathan protested as he started to his feet. Once he stood up his eyes got wide and his mouth dropped open also. "No, please tell me that you didn't do that." He said those same words back to Earlyman.

They both quickly grabbed their guns, checked the bullet chamber, and saw that one shot had been fired from each of their guns. "Man we didn't!" They both said at once.

Billy Ray and Suzy Ann Parker where propped up in bed with bullet holes in their heads. Their eyes were wide open and they had a big blue bowl of popcorn between them. There they both were as dead as can be. "Listen man, we did not kill these people. Now I don't know how this happened but all I do know is we didn't do this." Jonathan said.

"That might be true but with these guns on us and them having been fired and all, you would never be able to convince a jury of that fact. Anyhow we don't know what happened when we blacked out." Earlyman said.

"Listen, let's get up out of here and don't touch one single thing." Jonathan replied. The young men both tucked the guns in their waist lines, wiped everything down for fingerprints, and bolted out the back door.

"We will toss these guns in the bottom of the lake and we will make a promise never to talk to anybody about this experience," Earlyman said, now using his best wisdom. They had stayed up that entire night walking and thinking about what had happened back at that old cabin. Before they knew anything, the sun was coming up on the horizon bringing in the dawn of a new day. They continued to walk with swiftness on the dirt road that led from the cabin trail as they plotted and planned. The young men stopped to take a break.

As they bent over to rest, it seemed as if out of nowhere a car pulled up behind them. "Hey, what you boys doing up this time of morning?" It was Mr. James, returning home from working the overnight shift at the mines in Mulberry.

"Oh nothing, sir. Just thought that we would get us an early morning run in." Jonathan said.

"Well if you boys are finished with your run then hop on in and I'll give you a lift on down to the end of the road. Maybe we will stop in at Mildred's and grab us some breakfast and a cup of coffee." Mr. James said.

"Oh no thank you, sir. We're not hungry." Jonathan blurted out.

"Oh sure you are, hanging out with that big partner of yours. I have never seen a time when Earlyman was not hungry. Isn't that right, son?"

"Ah, yes sir." Earlyman responded. As they were getting in the car Jonathan nudged him in the side as they both made their way into the back seat; the front seat was covered with books and papers.

Mr. James pulled into Mildred's Diner and as usual it was filled with the early morning breakfast crew that had either got off of work or was on their way to work. He pulled up to the parking lot space that was closest to the front door. "Come on guys; let's see what Mildred got cooking up on the grill. My, my, my, that sure does smell good to me." Mr. James said as he quickly opened the car door and made his way to the entrance of the diner. "Come on, come on!" He yelled back at the boys.

"We will be there in a minute." Jonathan called out as they both fell behind.

"Okay, suit yourself; I am going to get in here and get my grub on." Earlyman said as Mr. James walked on and into the diner."

"Man, what are you doing? As a matter of fact, what are we doing? We cannot be here with him; he'll ask us a lot of questions. You know how nosey Mr. James is. He is not settled with the fact that we was up this time of morning running and working out. You should have never accepted his invitation to breakfast. And besides you know that he saw us standing right down the road that leads to the path of the cabin." Jonathan said.

"Well he would have saw us anyways since he pulled up out of nowhere," answered Earlyman.

"Yeah but if we would not have accepted this ride then he probably would have forgot."

"Anyhow there's no need crying over spilled milk." Earlyman said.

"Spilled milk: Is that what you call this? Brother, this situation is more like a leaking cow nipple."

Just as both of the young men started to walk in the diner, they noticed a homeless man standing out front, begging for change to get something to eat. The man had pure white skin and a head full of white hair. It appeared as if someone had bleached him or something. He had somewhat a milky or translucent pigmentation. His eyes seemed to be pink with deep red pupils. He appeared to be no more than forty years old. His clothes were well-worn and he must have had them on for quite a long time. His teeth were black, green and yellow. "Can you boys help me out with a hot cup of coffee?" He asked.

"Listen man, why don't you get a job." Earlyman said as he looked over at Jonathan, who reached into his pocket and pulled out a dollar. He bypassed Earlyman's hand and gave it to the homeless man.

The man looked at both of them and said, "Is that all that you can give a man who knows your deepest and darkest secrets?" The man cackled out a laugh and ran across the street. A city bus passed by and the man was gone.

"What in the world was that?" Jonathan asked.

"I don't know but did you hear what he said? Brother, we've been found out." Earlyman replied.

Maybe he's just making small talk or thinks that he is a fortune teller or something. Anyways we had better get in there before Mr. James comes out here. You know that his nosy old self ain't gonna let us off the hook that easy. So we may as well go in there and face the music." Both of the young men went into the diner where Mr. James was sitting, reading the morning newspaper, and sipping a cup of coffee.

Shawn R. Mosley

Chapter 13

It's All Bad

Mildred was a big-boned light-skinned African-American woman. She was not fat, just big. She had a pretty pair of hazel green eyes that made the male customers appreciate coming to her diner. The female customers would come there to see why the men were so anxious to patronize Mildred's place of business. The two young men sat at the table with Mr. James and he pulled the newspaper down from his face. Mildred walked over to the table with that big pleasant smile on her face and commented, "I see you have two more with you this morning?"

"Yes, that is correct," he answered. "Let me have two more cups of coffee and your famous biscuits and gravy with a side order of grits; and while you are at it, give me a warm up on this coffee." Mildred grabbed the cup from the table and poured the fresh coffee.

"Is there anything else?" she asked.

"No that will be all for now."

"Okay, coming right up." Mildred replied. She walked away with all the grace of a professional.

"Boy, that sure is some kind of woman," Mr. James said. "Now back to you two. Now you know that I don't believe for one single moment that you two was out this time of morning running and exercising. So now let's hear it. I want to know what you two was up too."

"That is the truth that we told you. Earlyman is planning to try out for a semi-pro football team in Tampa, so we got to get him in the best of shape." Just as Jonathan was finishing his explanation, Sheriff Boatwright walked in. Jonathan looked up and he felt his heart drop down to his stomach, or so it felt. At that very moment nothing that Mr. James said registered to him. It was as if the only person in the room was him and Sheriff Boatwright.

Mildred walked over to the sheriff. "What will you have this morning, Sir?"

"I would like a cup of decaf and one of those cinnamon rolls."

"Coming right up," she said. As Mildred walked away, the sheriff turned around and looked directly at Jonathan and Earlyman. It seemed as though he was looking directly into their eyes. Sheriff Boatwright never smiled and he always seemed to be suspicious of everybody. Now his eyes was on them. Mildred started back over to the sheriff holding the pot of coffee and at that moment his attention shifted off the boys and on to her. "Cream and sugar?" she added.

"No, I'll take it straight," he said.

Just as he started to sip on his coffee, his walkie-talkie went off. "*Sheriff Boatwright, come in.*"

"This is Sheriff Boatwright," he responded to the call on his walkie-talkie.

"*We have some disturbing news at the Parker Place. It appears that a neighbor went over to do the usual morning bible study and he knocked on the door and got no answer so he walked in that old cabin and he saw both Billy Ray and Suzy Ann sitting up in the bed just as dead as road kill.*"

"I'll be there directly in five or six minutes." Sheriff Boatwright looked over at the boys one last quick glance and rolled up off the stool that he was sitting on at the counter and wobbled toward the door.

"Hey Sheriff--you forgot your bill!" Mildred called out to him.

"Yeah I know I got kind of an emergency right now just put it on my tab and I'll pay it later." Sheriff Boatwright was a round and plump Southerner known by his friends as B.T. He was a good ole boy from the heart of Dixie known as a red neck. His personal beliefs was that blacks, Hispanics, and Jews were only put here to be servants to the supreme white race!

As Sheriff B.T. drove up to the cabin, he could see that the crime scene investigators had already taped off the area and was probing for some trace of evidence that would lead them in the right direction for a suspect. He got out of his car and walked over to one of the deputies. "So what kind of leads do we have so far?" The sheriff asked.

Before the deputy could answer, Mr. James drove up slowly with Jonathan and Earlyman in the back seat. "You boys sit right here; I want to go and check out what is going on back here. It must be something serious, seeing all those deputy cars out by the road." He got out of his vehicle and walked over to talk to one of the deputies as well. Both of the young men sat there speechless and hoped not to draw any suspicion to themselves.

"Man this is like living in a nightmare! I don't know how all of this happened but it sure was not in my plans at all," Jonathan said.

"Mine either!" Earlyman was in just as much shock as his friend was. "So do you think that they will ever be able to pin it on us?" he asked.

"Who knows man; these old racist white boys down here will not stop looking until they have some unfortunate black man hanging on the other end of a noose from a tall oak tree." Jonathan replied.

"I just hope that those unfortunate black men ain't us." Earlyman said. As they sat in the back seat they noticed that the coroners were putting the two covered corpses into the meat wagon. Mr. James came back to the car shaking his head from side to side.

"Boys, I can't believe it. Who in their right mind would go up in those people's house and kill them like that? That was the new Reverend and his wife; they just moved here to Medulla to help us black folk out.

"Reverend?" Earlyman was shocked.

"Yeah; didn't you read it in the newspaper that he and his wife had moved down here from Alabama to help generate grants and funds in the black community?"

"No, as a matter fact I heard the complete opposite" Earlyman said as he looked at Jonathan.

Mr. James backed up the car. "So what did you hear?" He asked as he looked in his rear-view mirror.

"Oh nothing worth talking about since the Reverend and his wife is now dead," Earlyman said.

"Well let me get ya'll back to the house," Mr. James replied as they drove away.

35

Shawn R. Mosley

Chapter 14

Everything is Crazy

"This is John Clark bringing you a C.B.S. breaking news report. Today in the small town of Medulla, two people were found dead in their home, each due to a single gunshot to the head. Investigators however have not made a positive identification of the suspect but eye witnesses report seeing two black men hanging out on to the path that led up to the house around 11:25 last night. These and more details tonight at 8. This is John Clark, C.B.S. News; now back to your regularly scheduled program."

Both men sat with their mouths open. "Listen man, they are on our trail. Somebody knows what we did." Earlyman panicked.

"Man we ain't done nothing but pass out on the floor." Jonathan said.

"Yeah but we woke up with two rounds fired out of our guns and two people dead. And what's worst, one of them just happened to be a preacher and the other was his wife. Not only are we going to get caught but we are going to burn in hell after they hang us." Earlyman said. "Jonathan you sure do know how to pick 'em. Them people are as far as the east is from the west from being racest or ku klux klan members. I am kicking myself for letting you talk me into going with you. I must be the stupidest man on planet earth." Earlyman continued to voice his frustration throughout the day. Jonathan knew that he was venting but he also knew that Earlyman was a true friend and together they would make it through this terrible situation.

The word spread quickly around Medulla of the tragic double homicide of the Reverend and his wife. And what made the news even worse was the fact that the investigators were looking for two black men. The racial tension was brewing; if the killers were not soon caught and dealt with, it was obvious that a race riot would take place. Many of the local white store owners stopped doing business with the blacks in their community. Blacks and whites walked down the streets but would pass and not greet each other. All the white customers that normally ate at Mildred's Diner stopped coming in and spent their money elsewhere. And it seemed as if that old racist sheriff B.T. Boatwright was not about to let up on his investigation until he had at least one black man in custody. He and his deputies were staking out all the black night clubs, bars and bootleggers. They set up road blocks and stopped every black man and ran warrant checks on them. Everyone that didn't have proper identification was taken in for questioning, which always ended with police brutality. It had gotten to the point that many of the wives would squeeze their black husbands tightly before they went off to work because they did not know if it would be their last time seeing each other.

For the first time in the relationship, things were uneasy between Jonathan and Brenda. She watched Jonathan pace the kitchen floor as he looked back and forth out of the window. In times past the moments that they shared were good, but lately they had become very stressful. Jonathan felt that he could share anything with her but this one he didn't quite understand himself. Besides, how could he tell her that all the tension that was going on in their town was because he was blinded by racism and had acted foolishly? How could he give an explanation that he would soon be wanted for murder and possibly spend the rest of his life in prison? He knew that old nosey Sheriff Boatwright was hot on his trail. His mind began to toss the many 'what ifs' around. "Jon, I really don't know what's up with you tonight but you are acting very strange," Brenda interrupted his thoughts.

"It's really nothing. I just got a lot on my mind." He said.

"Well let's go back out into the family room and watch some T.V.; maybe that will relax you a little bit." She said, trying to get him to loosen up a little.

Jonathan nodded as they finished up their sodas and went back into the family room. *Okay let me pull it together and relax.* Jonathan thought to himself, *I am cool; they will never be able to pin me and Earlyman to that murder. And even if they do find out, maybe I will get off on an insanity plea because this is some crazy mess. The only problem with that theory is they are not going to believe that Earlyman and I went crazy at the same time.* Brenda curled up on the couch with the remote control and as she laid her head on Jonathan's chest, she turned on the T.V.

"This is John Clark bringing you a special news report in the double homicide case of Reverend Billy Ray Parker and his wife, Suzy Ann." The image of a man's face came on the screen. *"Police said that this man can positively identify both of the black men who are believed to be suspects in this particular case."*

Jonathan took a look at the man on the T.V. screen and almost passed out. "Oh my God," He said out loud before he realized it. It was that ugly albino homeless man from the diner. Was it true that he really had something on them? It seemed like his whole world was crashing down around him. And what about his beautiful Brenda? He knew that if he got caught that they would have to be separated for a long period and maybe even forever.

As Jonathan sat there and tried to figure out what he was going to do, there was a sudden knock at the door and he jumped to his feet. "I'll get it, Babe; you just sit still." Once he got to the door, he saw Earlyman standing outside with a look of overwhelming fear in his eyes.

"Come on man. They got Mr. James and they're beating him up bad."

"Who?" Jonathan asked.

"I don't know nothing except he got caught by an angry mob of white folks. They seem to think that he knows something and won't talk. So they say that there're going to make him pay." Both Jonathan and Earlyman headed out the door; Brenda tried to stop them but it was to no avail.

Shawn R. Mosley

Chapter 15

Evil Hearts of Men

By the time Jonathan and Earlyman got to Mr. James' place, all they saw was a trail of blood leading up the street; they followed the trail and realized that he had been tied to a car bumper and slowly dragged up and down the streets. When they saw him, his knees were nothing but chunks of raw flesh and bone. His face was swollen to the point that he was nearly unrecognizable. The warm blood poured down his face as the angry mob took a rope and threw it over the branch of a tall oak tree. "I heard that the sheriff had been called." Earlyman whispered. But there was no trace of him in sight. Mr. James was placed on the back of a horse wagon. There was about twenty five to thirty men standing around with shot guns in case anybody wanted to try to step in and try to save him. The horrific scene made both men want to vomit.

"Man could we be the cause of all of this?" Jonathan asked. As they both crouched down in the hedges out of harm's way, Jonathan said, "I've got to stop them," and motioned toward the gruesome scene.

Earlyman reached out and grabbed him in one quick motion. "You're dying with him ain't going to stop that redneck mob, you know? You will just be another dead black man. It's too late." They watched the men stand Mr. James up, put the noose around his neck, and push the wagon from underneath him. Their hearts dropped as he hung from that tree: An innocent man had now lost his life because of a misunderstanding. The evil hand of racism had reached out its ugly grasp and it was not about to stop anytime soon.

As Jonathan and Earlyman made their way back through the dark streets, they noticed a moving shadow up ahead by a tree. The street lights up the road shone down on a man of about five feet four inches tall. The closer they got to the tree the more clear the image of the man became to them. Finally they saw who it was: the homeless man from the diner. " Hey man, that's him! That's the guy from the news, you know--the one from Mildred's place. Come on, let's get him!" Jonathan said. They both took off after him.

The man looked up, saw them coming towards him, and without a moment's hesitation took off running at full speed: the chase was on. He took off with the speed of a professional football player and both young men soon realized that they did not stand a chance of catching up to him. He was jumping fences, crawling through sewer pipes, and running through people's yards; he was totally committed to getting away.

"Okay he's coming to the canal; it's a dead end for him. I think we've got him." Jonathan said. Just as they were closing in, the homeless man took a giant leap across the rushing canal and cleared it by at least three feet more. Both of the young men ran to the edge of the forceful waters and stopped right in their tracks. They stood there breathing heavily. From the other side of the canal the man turned around, smiled, and waved at the young men, then took off running again. There was no use trying to catch him. *How did a broke down homeless man have such ability? He ran so fast and made such a difficult jump seem to be so easy. In what seemed like a few seconds he just left us in the dust*, Jonathan thought to himself.

"If only we could have caught up to him then we could have found out what he knows. That way at least we would know what we are up against." Earlyman said. They continued walking back toward Brenda's house, too tired to have any kind of conversation. They both kept walking in silence and finally came into view of Brenda's house. "Oh my God: No!" They both said at once, breaking the silence. They saw the tall wooden cross burning on the front lawn. Directly behind the cross was a lot of smoke coming from the house. At that very moment, fear gripped their hearts.

Jonathan quickly reached down and grabbed a brick from the ground. He rushed over to the family room and threw it into the window, which broke the plate glass. "Come on man help me out." They both took off their shirts and wrapped them around their noses and made their way into the broken window. The house was burning and pieces of the burnt ceiling fell in front of them as they made their way through. They called out Trudy and Brenda's names but there was no answer.

As they walked through the smoke-filled hallways, Earlyman tripped over something and fell. He got to his feet and reached down to find out what had tripped him up. To his shock and surprise it was a body. "Hey man, I think I found one."

"Get her and drag her out of here," Jonathan said. Earlyman reached down, grabbed the body, and started to make his way through the burning house.

"I'll find the other one." Jonathan yelled back as he carefully moved through the flames. He pressed his way throughout the house as it became more difficult for him to breathe because of the thick smoke. He got down on his knees and began to crawl. Finally he made his way to a room with another window broken out. Through it the street lights cast a reflection into the room and he could see a lifeless figure of what appeared to be a person. The closer he got to the figure the more he realized that it was Brenda, slumped in a corner by the window ledge. He picked her up and dove through the open window with her. In his haste to exit he did not see that she had a gunshot wound through the heart. Once he hit the ground with her body, he gasped for air; he regained composure and saw the bullet hole in her chest. Jonathan cuddled her head in his arms and rocked back and forth, not saying a word as tears of crushing pain rolled down his face. He looked over across the yard and saw Earlyman using his shirt to cover Trudy's face. The young men could hear sirens blaring in the distance.

"Come on Jon; we've got to get out of here." Jonathan just sat there in a trance. "Come on, Bro. She's gone and there ain't nothing that you can do." Earlyman pleaded. "We don't need the questioning of the law at a time like this; come on, let's get out of here." After Jonathan kissed Brenda on the lips and folded her arms over her chest, they both ran off with hearts full of grief and confusion.

People who had been neighbors and had lived peacefully together for years were now at war with each other. The hatred between the two races of people, blacks and whites, was boiling with fury. The violence and looting had gotten so bad until nobody was safe anymore. From a distance, Earlyman and Jonathan hid out and watched a gang of black men pull a white family from a car and kill them execution style by tying a bandana around their eyes and shooting each of them in the back of the head. They saw white men in trucks drive through a parking lot and run over as many black people as they could.

What gives mankind the right to destroy God's most beautiful creation? Don't we know that one day we will all have to answer to God for our prejudices and racism? When will we learn that God only made one race--the human race--and he loves us all just the same?

Shawn R. Mosley

Chapter 16

The Secret Exposed

The rundown shack somehow still had cold running water in it. It was next door to the house that Mr. James used to live in. After that night at Brenda's house, Jonathan and Earlyman tried to avoid contact with the outside world as much as possible. After all, they believed within themselves that they were the cause of the devastation in their town. They knew that if they were ever found to be the cause of all the trouble that the town of Medulla was going through, the people of both races would turn on them.

But they both knew that the homeless man was about to spill the beans on them by telling it all. It was vitally important that they caught up with him before Sheriff Boatwright got the chance to take him out on a man hunt because they knew that the finger would end on them. The old shack wasn't much to look at but it provided a place for them to hide out in for a while. It had been a long time since Jonathan had had a nightmare vision. *Maybe because I am living in a nightmare*, he thought to himself. His mind continued to wander and he realized that he seemed to lose everything that had ever mattered to him. He reflected on the place that he found himself in when he was stabbed while in prison. He remembered the peace of mind that he had felt along with the amazing beauty that was beyond words. He started to do a heart examination of how his innocence was stolen through Erma's death. *The hatred and bitterness against an entire race is because of the hatred of a few.* He thought to himself. *The hatred that others released caught me up in its ugly web. Now it controls and sickens me daily. All of this that's going on is a result of my hatred.* He looked over in the corner of the room and stared upon his only true friend in the world. Earlyman was propped up against an old fire place, sleeping fitfully. Jonathan began to drift off into dream land as well.

"That's them right there, Sheriff." Jonathan and Earlyman were awakened by the sound of growling dogs and bright flashlights shining into their eyes. The homeless man and Sheriff Boatwright were standing in front of them. Jonathan and Earlyman tried to get to their feet but they were both struck across the face with the butt of a shot gun.

"Are you absolutely sure that these are the men who you saw coming out of Billy Ray and Suzy Ann Parker's house?"

"Yep sir; absolutely, positively sure." The homeless man

responded.

"Please Sheriff, let me explain." Jonathan tried to intervene on his own behalf and all of a sudden he felt a hard blow against the side of his face.

"Listen here, you lil' nigga Jigga Boo: if I wanted you to talk then I would have asked you. I am gonna show you little nigglets about causing all this friction in my town," the sheriff growled. He looked over at the homeless man then gave a look to one of his deputies.

"Hey you, get out of here." The deputy said.

"But what about my reward money?"

The sheriff reached into his wallet, pulled out a twenty dollar bill, and gave it to the man. "Now listen here you lil' light pigmented nigger, I best not hear one word about these boys or you'll be next. Now go on, get out of here."

The albino man looked at the two bleeding men one last time and took off out the door. "So do you want us to take care of them now, Sheriff?" One of the other deputies asked.

"No; we're going to take them back to the cabin in the middle of the cornfield. We are going to do to them exactly what they did to that Reverend and his wife," Sheriff Boatwright answered.

"Turn over on your stomachs before we put a bullet in you right now." The deputy said to Jonathan and Earlyman. Both men were handcuffed and shackled together as they lay there on the floor of the old shack. They were quickly assisted off the floor and escorted out into the pitch black darkness of the night. Lined up in a row outside was what appeared to be at least six deputy patrol cars. They were thrown into the back seat of one of them and were soon back on that same old dirt road where it all began.

"Hey bro. Thank you for being a true friend." Jonathan said with tears in his eyes.

Earlyman looked back. "If I had to pick somebody to die with my brother it would have been you." "Like Donna and Erma--best friends until death do us part." Tears were rolling down both of their faces but there was a smile of brotherly love between them also.

The car that they were riding in turned off the dirt road and headed towards the cabin; from the time the men were taken out of the back seat of the car they were beaten with billy clubs and the butt end of shotguns. They were knocked to the ground in the haste of being yanked out of the car. At one point Earlyman shouted, "Hey man, you still alive?"

"Yeah man I am still in the land of the living." They continued to call to each other periodically, communicating through much pain and agony.

"Come on let's put these niggers' lights out." The sheriff said.

The deputies pulled both of the men through the back door of the cabin and on down the hallway. When they got to the Parker's bedroom, they were thrown to the floor. Two of the deputies drew their side arms and held them to the young men's heads. "Say your prayers, niggers," one of them said. Suddenly the room began to spin around and both Earlyman and Jonathan found themselves losing consciousness. They faded in and out helplessly until they went out completely.

Shawn R. Mosley

Chapter 17

Another Chance At Life

"Where are we? Are we dead?" Earlyman asked. Both he and Jonathan seemed to have regained their composure. They looked around the place: There was no Sheriff Boatwright; there were no deputies. The room was perfectly neat. The guns were laying in the middle of the floor and there were no bullet casings on the floor.

Could it be? Jonathan thought to himself. He reached up to feel his face and found not one bruise was on it. As they stood up, he looked at the bed and saw that it was made up nice and neat with the covers pulled up over the pillows. He heard a noise and turned; to his utter shock there was that homeless man standing behind them, but this time there was a very bright ray of light glowing all around him.

And right before Jonathan's and Earlyman's very eyes, the homeless man began to transform.

He began to grow taller and became more muscular; his face lit up with a ray of beauty and strength. His garments became white in splendor and his eyes were as flames of fire. From his back a pair of wings began to spread from one end of the room to the other. Jonathan and Earlyman fell to the floor as dead men. "My name is Gabriel and I stand in the presence of the God of all creation. I am His messenger." The angel said. "Stand to your feet," he commanded. The men struggled to their feet because the glory of God was so strong in the room that it was nearly impossible to stand up. "I was sent to tell you that you are commanded to go and proclaim the things you have both seen and heard. Tell every man, everywhere. Let them all know about the destruction that is not only to come upon the town of Medulla but also on the whole world. Men must repent and stop despising what God has made. Everything that the Lord has made is beautiful. Our God is a God of variety and this includes people. Who has a right to despise His handy work?"

Both men stood and trembled under the power of God as the angel Gabriel continued to speak. "The place and the people that you just saw were all created by God created within the span of one hour, yet He made it appear to you as if it had been many days. But now He is about to return you back to the life that you both know and love. But you must go back with these things: forgiveness and love. God is going to give you both a new mouth." At that point the angel took two burning coals and placed one in the mouths of each young man. They felt no

49

pain to them but something that looked like the ghosts of themselves left each of their bodies. The first had a face of hurt, the second a face of anger, the third a face of rage and the last a face of low self-worth. Each ghostly personality took with it the influence that it once had in the lives of each man; it was as if they had been cleansed in their very souls.

The angel turned to Jonathan. "In order for me to close the book on your past Jonathan, your eyes must bare this unbearable sight one more time." Jonathan closed his eyes and the nightmare vision began to play through his mind:

Jonathan is running through the woods. "Hey boy come back here." The sheriff screams out behind him. He ignores the command and just keeps on running. He hears the sound of the barking dogs and right there standing in the mist of the tall oak trees he sees the look of disgust on the faces of the deputies. Three of them are vomiting while the others look as if they had seen a ghost. Before any of them could react, Jonathan is upon them. Erma and Donna are there, sitting under the tree with their stomachs cut open. Their insides are gone and their bowels have been replaced with baby dolls. Written on a white canvas in their blood was a sign: "Stay in a child's place, niggers."

In that moment, Jonathan stood outside of himself and he saw evil ghost personalities of fear, racism, murder, rebellion, deep hurt, rage, distrust, and unforgiveness enter his body. He had been ten years old. Little did he know back then that those same evil spirits would make many attempts to control and even kill him throughout the years. Now at the age of 21, God was driving out all of those wicked forces through the anointing of those burning hot coals.

Tears ran down his face and Earlyman's as well; beautiful bolts of color from the angel's hands began to shoot into them and released a feeling of joy and bliss that either had never experienced before. "This is the new life of God that brings an awakening to your very souls. This life is eternal. The Beautiful One wants you to experience it." *Who is the beautiful one?* They both thought to themselves; they never opened their mouths to say a word.

"I AM," came the reply from the door; in walked the most beautiful man that they had ever seen. Everything about this Beautiful One reached out with warmth and love. Gabriel covered his face with his wings and bowed down to the ground. Both young men felt a voice in their hearts cry out: "Do you receive me Jonathan? Do you receive me Earl?" Neither was distracted by the fact that this One used Earlyman's real name.

They both cried out and confessed in unison, "Yes! I receive you!" They both found themselves on their knees trembling and constantly repeating "I receive you. I receive you." Their eyes were closed tightly but when they opened them, the angel and the Beautiful One were gone. It was 12:35 in the morning. Both men looked at the bed one more time and saw that it was in fact made to perfection. They embraced.

"Nobody would ever believe it." Jonathan said. They both walked out the back door of the cabin and were very glad to see that cornfield that led them back to the dirt road. As they walked back down the old dusty road, their hearts were rejoicing. They passed by Trudy and Brenda's house and noticed that the car was in the driveway and there was no fire damage. Their house looked as peaceful as ever. There was no angry mobs roaming the streets burning crosses. Finally they made their way down to the end of the road and saw Mr. James as he pulled out the drive way on his way to work. He had worked the same overnight shift for years.

He saw the boys and slowed down. "Hey where are ya'll going this time of night? Shouldn't you guys be at home sleep?"

Old man Mr. James, nosy as ever, Jonathan thought to himself. But he was so happy to see the man in his car and not dangling from the end of a rope.

Life in the town of Medulla was about to change in a wonderful way. And God was going to use Jonathan and Earlyman to help carry it out.

51

Shawn R. Mosley

Chapter 18

The New Life

Trudy and Brenda

Trudy was up to her same old ways. "Hey Brenda; I need you to watch the house for me tonight. I have a date."

"So, who is the lucky guy this time?" Brenda asked.

"His name is Eric Mattson and he is an investment broker at a local law firm. It has been said that he is one of the top brokers in the state." Trudy answered.

"So mom, how did you meet him?"

"Well, do you remember when I flew out to Scottsdale Arizona with Mark Jackson, that defense attorney?"

"Yes Momma, I vaguely remember that."

"Well it just so happened that him and Mark are college buddies. They both went to Morehouse. For some reason they get together for their class reunion and afterwards fly out to Arizona for a week of golf and relaxation."

"I thought that you and Mark was still seeing each other." Brenda said.

"Now there you go, prying again. What you need to do is mind your own business." Trudy responded with much sarcasm.

"Well excuse me. I was just concerned in case he just happens to call and asks where you were. Then I would know what to tell him."

"Child, please. That man ain't gonna hardly call."

Brenda asked, "How do you know?"

"Because Mark is on his anniversary, celebrating ten years of marriage with his wife."

"Okay mom; I don't think I want to know anymore." Brenda said.

"Girl, you better use what the good Lord gave you. Anyhow a man is supposed to take care of a woman and in other ways we take care of them. They give us what we want: cars, houses, diamonds, and lots of money. And we give them what they want: our time, and if we want to keep them hanging on, then we give them a little bit more." Trudy grabbed her Gucci bag and slid on her high heels that matched her dress. "So how do I look honey?"

"Absolutely marvelous." Brenda responded. With a wink, Trudy threw a lock of hair behind her ear and headed out the door.

Billy Ray and Suzy Ann

"Suzy Ann, I'll tell you what: If the Lord had not told me to take you to Lakeland to be with your sister I sure would not have done it. I have been trying to talk to your family about the Lord for quite a few years now and they just don't seem to want to hear it," Billy Ray said as he drove down the dusty highway heading home.

"Well that's just because you don't see what's going on inside of them. You know that God's word is like a seed in the ground; if you keep on watering it then it will eventually grow inside Loretta and Randy. And besides, how about the work the Lord caused you to do in their neighbors? You need to think about that. Bobby Gene and Linda Sue use to have the hootinest, lootinest corn whiskey parties that I have ever seen before. They got rid of their distillery and quit the drinking, and now they are both serving the Lord. I'd say that's not bad Billy Ray, not bad at all."

"You know my little wild flower, I never even thought of that. You are one heck of a good woman." he said.

"Well I don't reckon I did too bad myself." Suzy Ann smiled. They continued their journey down the highway, holding hands and enjoying the scenery. All the Florida pine trees were blowing from side to side. Standing on the side of the road was a five point Buck that looked as if it was going to dart out into the traffic. Farther down the road they saw a small volt of turkey vultures ripping away on an opossum carcass. Suddenly a very sharp pain shot through Suzy Ann's lower back. "Oooh!" she groaned loudly.

"Honey, what's wrong? Is everything all right?" Billy Ray asked.

"I am just fine," she lied. "Stop worrying so much."

Mr. James

Now where is that big pretty fine half-breed woman that usually works this area of town? Mr. James thought to himself as he drove aimlessly, looking to pick up a prostitute on Cherry Lane. The lust of uncontrollable urges burned in the loins of James Roberson as he drove through the streets of Medulla, looking for the young woman he had spotted earlier that day. The nagging appetite for sexual fulfillment overwhelmed him with its screaming desires. *I can't let the pastor of the church see me driving up and down this old road. After all this is Drugville, U.S.A.* James Roberson was a prominent leader in the community; he worked alongside the mayor of the city of Lakeland. He was also the head deacon in the First Missionary Baptist Church. His sphere of influence gained him much clout and respect. He was considered to be a decent man and an all-around good human being. But he had a secret that could ruin and destroy his reputation. The people would no longer look up to him. *There she is, right there.* He slowly pulled to the curb. "Hey sweetie; what are you doing all of that walking for?" He hollered out to the young lady who looked to be in her mid-twenties or early thirties. "Do you need a ride?"

"Yeah Daddy were you headed?" She responded.

"Anywhere you want to go. How many roses will it take to make a young lady like you happy?" He was talking roses but meant money.

"Forty roses will make this girl very happy and we can hang out for thirty minutes. But eighty roses will make this girl extremely happy and the happier I get the happier I will make you." She said. The young lady was the typical girl of the streets who had been hardened by life, guilt, and shame. She forced another smile through the eyes of hate, hurt, and pain as she climbed in beside him. He gave her some money and they drove off.

Mildred

At five Friday evening, Mildred Thatcher locked the door of the diner and walked towards the black on black Thunderbird. *Thank God it's Friday; I can get my smoke on tonight. I'll let David and Kathy open up the restaurant for me tomorrow. I wonder if I can get a hold of Tookie and see if he will sell me an ounce of weed. I can smoke a little bit and then sell some of it,* she thought to herself as she turned the key and unlocked the vehicle. Mildred's brother Tookie was one of the biggest drug dealers in the Ponce de Leon housing projects in Tampa, which was about an hour away from Medulla. He had bought the restaurant for her as well as some other businesses. He used them as a front to launder his drug money. Mildred was a successful small business owner with one major problem: She loved to sell marijuana and would get high on her own supply. Nobody knew her little secret except a few of her friends that she partied with. As a matter of fact, all of her friends were business people as well so she reasoned in her own mind that it was okay because they all took care of their responsibilities first. *After all, we ain't doing the heavy stuff like heroin or cocaine; it was just marijuana,* she thought to herself. *Yeah, I'll call my brother when I get home and he will give me what I have been waiting for all week long. After working so hard all week long there is nothing wrong with a girl sitting down with a glass of wine and a joint to get relaxed. Look out weekend 'cause here I come!* She turned into her driveway, pushed the garage door opener, and pulled in.

Shawn R. Mosley

Chapter 19

The Reason Why

Jonathan and Earlyman, who now preferred to be called Earl, had been spending a lot of time together since their strange encounter in the cabin in the middle of the cornfield. Life had taken on new meaning for the both of them; there was an urgency on the inside of them to begin making a difference in the lives of other people. The message was clear to them that they had had a divine encounter with Jesus, but what were they supposed to do with it? The reality that they were chosen kept a blaze of fire burning in their hearts. Now, nobody had to tell them to separate themselves and pray; it came natural to them.

As they would pray, nothing else seemed to matter: Not food, water, the doorbell, the phone, absolutely nothing but getting to know God by way of prayer. One day as they were praying, a smoky mist filled the air and they were unable to stand in it. The next day as they were praying their bodies began to shake almost violently as rays of light moved through them. At times they both felt tremendous grief and sorrow as if they were experiencing the pains of the world. It was in these times when faces of men and women would appear before their eyes; the people they saw were often gritting their teeth with anguish and their demeanor was filled with upset. Neither young man knew what to do beyond continuing to pray, which they did.

The urge to go to church and talk to someone about what they were experiencing had crossed their minds. But how do you tell people about these kinds of things? After all, Jonathan had been in a church as a child and he had never heard anybody talk to him about these kinds of things. They shared their thoughts with one another and agreed that people would think of them as quacks ready for the looney house.

For thirty days they just kept on praying. They ate no food and only drank water. Soon it would all make sense to them.

The Black Mercedes Benz pulled up in front of the ranch-style red brick house. Tookie picked up his car phone and dialed the number. "Hey Sis, it's me. I'm just sitting outside in front of the house," he said.

"So Tookie, do you got some work with you or do you have to go and get it?" Mildred asked. She had been sitting around, waiting for him; she filled the time by sipping on a glass of wine.

"Girl, what's my name? As a matter of fact I think you spell it w.o.r.k.! To keep it one hundred I got you covered like that nightgown that you like to wear." He said, laughing.

"Okay, okay; I didn't want to inflate that ego of yours. It's no wonder Momma had to have a C-section when you were born. If your head got any bigger, you wouldn't be able to get into the garage!" As she continued to talk to him on the phone, the garage door opened up. He pulled in alongside her car and the garage door started to close. He walked into the house and there was Mildred, sitting on the couch in her favorite nightgown nursing a glass of wine watching *Wheel of Fortune* on television.

"Hey girl, what you got to eat? I got the munchies something serious." Tookie asked as he went toward the kitchen.

"Boy I know that you are trippin'; get out of those pots because I didn't hear you run a drop of water to wash your hands. I don't know where your hands been at," she said over her shoulder.

He reached into his waistband and threw her a Zip Lock bag half-full of marijuana. "Roll us up one, so then maybe you'll stop being so cranky." He reached into his backpack and pulled out a white powdery substance that was in the form of a cookie.

At first glance Mildred thought that they were sugar cookies. "Tookie, what do you got right there?" she asked.

"This is some new stuff around here that has people going crazy. Slow-Moe turned me on to it. And the girls will do anything for it. And I mean anything for it."

Mildred sat, puffed on the joint she had rolled as they talked, and then passed it to Tookie. "You mean people are buying that cookie looking stuff? What do you do with it: shoot it, snort it or smoke it? What?"

"Oh they take it and break it into little crumbs and put it on a beer can and smoke it," he answered.

"Bro, you trippin'. As long as I got weed I don't need none of that cookie dough."

"Now Sis, hear me and hear me good. You do not want to get caught up with this stuff. From what I see it ain't good. Me and Slow-Moe was standing on Nebraska Avenue and a man drove up to us with a washer and dryer in the back of his truck. Slow-Moe went to give the dude some dope for it but before he could get it cut up, the man's wife and three children came up saying that he had stolen all the furniture out of the house. Slow-Moe felt sorry for the lady and told the dude to get up out of there before he got mad. So old boy got into his truck and took off with his wife and children trailing behind him like they were on a high speed chase." Tookie said.

"It's got 'em going out like that?"

"Yeah, just like that. I am going to leave some of this stuff over here cause it ain't cool riding with this much on me. But I need you to promise me that if you decide to sell some of it you will save my money for me and I'll break you off some cash when I get it from you. Now let me show you how to cut it up and how much to sell it for." Tookie said. He began to show his sister how much to sell each customer and how to weigh it out on the triple beam scale. Tookie and Mildred sat there for about two hours smoking weed and sipping on glasses of wine. They were so both out of it until they decided that it would be good for Tookie to leave because he had to drive all the way back to Tampa. Mildred did not want him to be so high that he could not drive home. The only thing that kept going through Mildred's head were what Tookie told her about the new stuff: *Slow-Moe is clocking like five grand a day.* Tookie grabbed his car keys and he gave her two more Zip Lock bags full of the white cookie rock. He kissed her on the side of her face. "Baby girl, put that up for me and I am out of here," he said as he walked out the side door that led into the garage.

"Okay bro. You drive safely; after all, you're the only brother that I have. If anything was to happen to you, where would I get such good weed?" Mildred joked. Tookie got into his car and Mildred let up the garage door, then watched as he backed out and drove off. She stood in the doorway and thought to herself that she must be the luckiest person in the world to have such a cool and caring brother. After all, it had only been three years since their mom and dad had died in a plane crash on their way to Jamaica. The only thing that they had in this world was each other. They were both successful business owners and they had love for each other. *Life is so good*, she thought and let down the garage door.

Suzy Ann lay on the bed, tossing and turning. The pain in her lower back was almost unbearable. She lay next to Billy Ray, not wanting to disturb his sleep. For the last month she had been feeling pains here and there but she continued to think that it was nothing serious. But the pain had intensified until it was almost twenty times worse than it had been in the beginning. The fear of what could be happening to her gripped her heart. The constant thoughts of death began to torment her mind over and over again. *Was it cancer or some other dreadful disease? Are my kidneys finally reaching the point of shutting down? If only this pain would stop*, she thought. She knew that it was not going to be much longer before she would have to tell Billy Ray what was going on with her. As she continued to lay there, a warm tear rolled over the bridge of her nose. The light from the T.V. reflected off the pictures on the dresser. She also noticed the alarm clock on her nightstand. It was after one in the morning and she had not slept a wink all night long. *I don't want to die. How is he going to make it without me? He is such a good man to me. It is not fair for him to make such a big fuss over me. I can't tell him.* Finally the pain subsided enough for her to fade out.

As her consciousness continued to fade, the room where Suzy Ann was sleeping turned into a dimly lit hallway. In the distance she could see what appeared to be a four legged beast racing towards her bed. As it got closer, she noticed how large and red its eyes were. It had a body like an ape but there were fangs growing out of both sides of its mouth. The beast leaped from the floor and landed on the side of the bed; she then noticed its claws. She tried to scream but nothing came out. She tried to move away from it but she was paralyzed by the strong force of the beast's power and could not move. She felt the heat of its breath on her neck. All of a sudden, it spoke in a very frightening whisper. "I am going to kill you."

She closed her eyes very tight and in her mind she cried out, *Jesus save me!* Suddenly there was a loud scream and she slowly opened her eyes. The room was back to normal and everything was just as it had been earlier. She looked over at Billy Ray, who was still sleeping peacefully on his pillow. The pain was still very real but she managed to find some type of comfort as she snuggled up close to Billy Ray and finally dozed off into an uninterrupted sleep.

Early the next morning, Billy Ray was awakened by the sound of a rooster crowing outside on the fence. The sun was shining through an open window in the room across the hall. Billy Ray looked over at his wife and lifelong partner and smiled. *If anything ever happened to my sweet Suzy Ann I don't know what I would do*, he thought. He slowly got out of the bed and was very careful not to wake her. He quickly started to get dressed because he knew that he had a full day ahead of him. He had to meet with some townspeople as he often did to offer prayers for some families. He also had to meet some of the homeless people in the park so that he could conduct the weekly feeding program. Just before he was ready to walk out the door he decided that he would take one last look at his beautiful wife. *So peaceful and sweet*, he thought. He slowly leaned over to kiss her and as he did he noticed that she was as cold as a block of ice. Instantly his heart started to race. "Oh my God, no! Oh no, Oh no! No God; no God!" He screamed at the top of his lungs. He grabbed her hand and began to check for a pulse, but there was none. He took his head and placed it to her chest; the tears began to flow like a waterfall from his eyes because there was not even a small heartbeat. He slowly reached over and gently grabbed Suzy Ann's head in his arms and rocked back and forth, hoping that this moment was unreal.

Shawn R. Mosley

Chapter 20

What is Happening to My Hands

After the week of being shut away from the rest of the world in constant prayer and fasting, Jonathan heard a familiar voice that he remembered from back at the cabin. "It is me and I AM He." It was the unmistakable voice of the Beautiful One. "Get to that cabin right away! Someone cries out in so much pain until it breaks my heart. We will help them," the Beautiful One said.

"But what am I to do, Lord?" Jonathan asked.

"If you go then I will show you what must be done." The Lord said. Jonathan got up off his knees and started toward the door. The voice of the Lord called out, "Get Earl and take him with you!"

Jonathan turned to Earl and shouted out to him, "Come on let's go; He has need of us." Earl already knew who Jonathan was talking about and did not say a word; he just got up and immediately left with Jonathan back to the dirt road that led to the cabin in the middle of the cornfield. As both of the young men quickly walked, they exchanged few words. But the Lord spoke many words to them. *Your hands will burn with a sensation of extreme warmth, but do not be alarmed; it is me pouring out my virtue into them. Your bodies will remain here on earth while your spirits will ascend and descend back and forth from heaven, bringing portions of it into the earthly realm. The need of this world is for not earthly things but for heavenly things. I have chosen you both to bridge the gap between heaven and earth. I have never hidden anything from my friends, not even heaven. It has always been my desire for my friends to experience heaven on earth. And I call you friends.* Jesus continued to talk to the men as they turned off the dirt road onto the path that went into the cornfield. As they got closer to the cabin, their clothes began to blow in a whirlwind that surrounded them. *Look at the trees: there is no wind blowing through them. Look at the stalks of corn: there is no wind moving through them. But you can hardly stand the force of wind that surrounds you.* Both of the young men's minds were locked in a state of boldness that they had never known and they pressed on to accomplish their unknown mission.

In their minds it didn't matter what they was up against; all that mattered was that they were being obedient to the Master's voice and knew He would equip them for the task. Once they were outside the cabin, both of the young men heard the agonizing cries of Billy Ray coming from inside. "Why God? Why?" Billy Ray screamed out at the top of his lungs. The voice of God instructed both Jonathan and Earl to go inside. At this point Jonathan's palms were red and the burning sensation he had started to feel intensified.

Jonathan and Earl entered the cabin and walked to the back room and found Billy Ray with Suzy Ann's head in his chest; he was just rocking her back and forth, pleading out to God. Earl spoke first. "She is not dead, but only asleep."

"No son, she is gone; I have already checked her pulse and she is as cold as can be." Billy Ray responded.

"But she will rise again and you will receive your dead back to life," Earl continued.

"I know that I will see my beautiful Suzy Ann again in the resurrection." Before Billy Ray could finish, Earl grabbed hold and pulled him away from Suzy Ann's body.

Up until then, Jonathan had not said a word; he just looked up to heaven with tears streaming down his face. Then he finally spoke out. "Lord, let the life of this woman re-enter this body."

At that very moment all three of the men's spiritual eyes were opened and they saw what appeared to be a younger and more radiant version of Suzy Ann descending from the ceiling; it came very slowly and rejoined her body. Her eyes began to flutter and then they opened up wide as she sat up in the bed with her hands lifted up to heaven. "Glory to God, who was and is and is to come!" She sang out as if she were singing in a mass choir. Billy Ray fell to his knees and raised his hands toward heaven as he worshipped the Lord for the great things that He had done. "I was singing in the heavenly choir with so many of the wonderful saints and the angels. I was escorted around heaven by this pretty black woman. She seemed to be so happy as she told me about how God had finally healed her older brother from the pain of bitterness and racial hatred. What a wonderful storyteller she was. It was the most beautiful place that I had ever seen before, Billy Ray. Oh, the streets were of the purest gold and the big beautiful gate was a solid pearl. But the most beautiful of all the sights that I saw was the face of Jesus. The love in his eyes melts you to mush. No one can stand in His presence until he invites them to. It's the power of His word that causes us to stand upright. He told me that you needed me and asked me to come back because one of his fellow servants was calling for my return. Jonathan and Earl were both kneeling down at the foot of the bed with their hands folded and heads bowed in humble adoration. They were thanking God for the miracle that he had performed in their midst. Without saying a word to the Parkers, they rose to their feet to walk out the door. "Jonathan!" Suzy Ann called out, "Wait just a minute.

As I was escorted out the gate, the pretty little black woman stopped me as we walked past the crystal sea. She told me that you would be here when I returned to this world. She told me that you can now enter into the gate."

Then all of a sudden the thought hit Jonathan like a ton of bricks: *Erma!* he said to himself. He looked at the Parkers as they held one another, smiled and headed out the door with Earl. Billy Ray ran out behind them. "Hey, would you like to stay for dinner?" He shouted. But by the time he got to the porch, they were already gone. Right where he was standing, he fell on his knees again and Suzy Ann came out behind him. They both made a vow to God that they would do everything in their power to show the people of Medulla the power of God in an even greater measure.

Shawn R. Mosley

Chapter 21

Dirty Old Man Made Clean

The black car pulled over to the side of the curb. "You get out of this car, you old thieving tramp," Mr. James yelled at the woman who he was literally kicking out of his car with his foot. The woman fell down in a water puddle on the side of the road. "The next time I see you I am gonna have my gun with me and I will blow your brains out."

"You didn't say that when you promised to give me forty dollars for your pleasure. All you tried to pay me was a measly five dollars. You must have lost your whole mind old man," she yelled as Mr. James drove off. The young lady sat there on the side of the road with tears rolling down her big beautiful lifeless eyes. "I am so tired of this life. I am nothing. I have got more miles on my body than I-95. No man is ever going to love me for who I am." She looked at her knees and they were skinned and bruised. She reached over into the puddle of rain water and began to wash her knees. Then all of a sudden she took her hands and dashed the water all over her face and body. *I feel so unclean. There is nobody who care about me or who will ever love me,* she thought to herself. Finally, she got up off the ground and with her shoes in her hands, started walking. In her heart she felt less than human. She had so cheaply sold her most valuable assets. How could she live with the fact that the thing that was supposed to be shared with someone special on her wedding night was abused by any man who had money to buy it. *I am just an object, a piece of meat,* she thought. Everything that was once good in her life had been stolen from her through a drug habit. For her, life had been unkind and she could think of no one or nothing that would deliver her from the misery of it.

Her mind began to reflect back to when she was a little girl and her momma used to twist her hair into pig tails. "Girl, I can't help it because you are so tender-headed. But you gonna sit still and let me finish your hair," she would say. "Toney, bring me that Royal Crown hair grease from up in the medicine cabinet in the bathroom." She continued to reflect. *Old Toney. If my brother was still alive then I would have someone here who would at least understand me. May he and momma rest in peace.* She had given up on life because she felt all alone in the world. Something had to change but she did not know if it was at all possible. The young woman continued on her way down the old dusty road. From behind her she heard the roar of a truck engine. She quickly reached into her bra to see if she still had the hundred dollars that she had stolen from Mr. James, wallet when he wasn't watching her. She could feel that it was still there. *Well if this is another trick pulling up behind me then I can pass on him because I don't need the money right now,* she told herself.

The truck began to honk its horn at her. She almost did not turn around to see who it was but at the last minute decided to take a peek over her shoulder. Thats when she heard the countriest white woman that she had ever heard. "Hey, where you reckon you heading off to, carrying them there shoes in your hand?" the woman asked. *Oh no; not one of them.* She thought to herself. The woman continued talking at her. "Come on, hop in, and I will give you a lift to where you are going." *Well maybe I can get her to drop me off to the dope man's house.* She turned around and walked back to the passenger side of the truck to get in. "Hey my name is Suzy Ann, but you can call me Sue." The driver said.

"Hello; my name is Cammi, but you can call me Chocolate," the young lady replied as she extended her hand out to Suzy Ann.

"Well I will just call you Cammi, how 'bout that? Suzy Ann asked.

No she didn't just do that! The young woman thought to herself with a whole lot of bad attitude. "Now the reason that I picked you up is because the Lord told me to." Suzy Ann said. *Now I thought I was going to the crack house but somebody ought to take this white woman to the quack house. Here it is she driving around talking to Jesus and stuff and she thinks he is talking back. If that ain't crazy then I don't know what is,* Cammi thought. "He told me about the pain and abuse that you went through when your mother and brother was still alive. He also told me how you were raped by your uncle. The Lord told me to let you know that He heard your cry" Suzy Ann said.

"Wait a minute old lady; you can just let me out of this truck right now! You don't know nothing about me. Nothing! There ain't no God nowhere. And anyhow who have you been talking to about me?! And don't give me that junk about you been talking to Jesus either." Suzy Ann's words were so true that they caught Cammi by surprise. The demons that she suppressed for years, that she had refused to deal with, were right there staring her in the face.

"Cammi, God said that you are forgiven and He loves you. Your brother Toney and your mother Arlena both told me to look after you. God told me that I would find you walking on this road today."

"What do you mean my momma and my brother talked to you?" Cammi asked.

"It may be hard for you to believe but the other night I after I got in bed to go to sleep I woke up in heaven; I would have stayed there if my husband had not prayed me back!" Suzy Ann shared. This was a very awkward moment for Cammi because she had never experienced anything like that before. But in her heart she knew it was all true. At that very moment she broke down and began to cry bitter tears. They pulled to the side of the road; Suzy Ann reached over and embraced Cammi as only a mother could. Their different worlds came together under one God, ministering healing to different races by love. At that very moment color was not even a factor. The pain that Cammi had carried around all of her life was finally being dealt with by someone she least expected. The tears flowed like a river and ended in her giving her life to Jesus.

Shawn R. Mosley

Chapter 22

This is Some Strange Stuff

It was a beautiful Sunday morning. Awakened by the crow of the rooster that was sitting on the fence outside of his window, Mr. James rolled over and out of bed. He knew he had to get ready for his regular Sunday morning routine: he would get up and fix himself a cup of coffee, go upstairs and pick out one of his favorite suits that he kept in his special suit closet, pull out his noticeable cross that he liked to hang down over his neck tie, and get ready for Sunday morning church service. Going to church was not something that he did from his heart to honor GOD. He was the head Deacon at the First Missionary Baptist Church. He believed that what you did Monday through Saturday night did not matter, as long as you made it to church on Sunday morning. He believed in doing good deeds towards those he thought to be decent people was the right way; on the other hand, he thought prostitutes and drug heads all deserved whatever bad fate they got coming to them. He never once considered that his sleeping around with such individuals made him as wrong as they were. He boasted in

the fact that he had been a member of the NAACP, a 33rd degree Mason and a faithful church going member for more than 30 years. As he stood there looking in the mirror tying his neck tie, a face of a woman appeared in the mirror and quickly faded. "Oh my goodness, I need to put on my glasses; I must be getting senile in my old age." He walked over to the drawer where he kept a lot of different pairs of eye glasses. He grabbed a pair that had wire earlobe rings and put them on. *Nope, these are not the ones*, he thought to himself. After going through about three or four of the wrong pair, he finally found the right ones. "Now that's more like it," he said to the empty room. Mr. James walked back over to the mirror and looked into it as he continued to get dressed. He dropped a cuff link on the floor; he bent down to pick it up and as he stood upright saw clearly a pregnant young lady holding her stomach in the mirror. He quickly turned around to see if anybody was there, but saw no one. He turned back and the only reflection in the glass was his own. "There is some scary stuff going on up in here," he said out loud. *I had better lay off that E&J Brandy*, he thought.

"Come here, you old nigga bed wench! Don't you run from your massa. Bring your little black hide here and serve your massa."

"Please massa please no! Don't do this to me!"

The voices of the white slave owner and black slave girl began

71

to fill the room. It was all too crazy for Mr. James to handle: his head began to spin and sweat began to now seep through his pores. "I must be losing my mind! I think I'll pour me a stiff drink." He went downstairs, walked over to the kitchen cabinet, retrieved a bottle of liquor, and poured a half shot glass full. As he attempted to put it up to his lips, the room opened up to totally new surroundings.

There was a young white man who looked to be about 36 years old and he was striking a young black slave girl across the face with the back of his hand. The man had torn the shoulder off her blouse as she ran around the room; she looked as if she feared for her life. "Get here right now, nigga wench" the slave owner said. Finally he caught up to the woman and began to tear off the rest of her clothes and proceeded to rape her as he continued striking her across the face.

Mr. James rushed over to stop the man from assaulting the slave girl. "Hey man, you can't do that. Stop it you hear?" Mr. James said. The constant abuse continued to play itself out. Mr. James went to strike the younger man with a closed fist, but just before he landed the fierce blow, the man turned around to look at him: Mr. James saw his own face!

"So you gonna hit me now?" Mr. James saw himself. He was the rapist and the slave girl who lay beneath him looked up; it was Cammi. Her throat was cut from ear to ear.

"Why didn't you stop him from killing me?" Cammi asked him.

He staggered back and fell into the Lazy Boy recliner. As soon as his rear hit the seat, the room returned to normal. *What in the world was that? This is one of the most frightening mornings that I have ever experienced in my life*, he thought. Somehow he still had the shot glass in his hand; he swallowed what was in it without wasting a drop. After wiping his mouth, he grabbed his Bible and headed out the front door for church.

As he drove down the road, he looked to the left; out by the cornfield there was a sign:

NO PEACE NO GOD, KNOW GOD KNOW PEACE

He was still very shaken up from what had taken place back at his house and he knew at that moment peace was the last thing he had. As he drove on, he saw the dirt road entrance that led to the cabin, along with another sign:

Let GOD heal your heart and give you peace.

There was an arrow pointing toward the cabin. *What does this old stinking world know about peace and GOD and all that stuff? I know the man upstairs. I've been a deacon for over 30 years; it looks like another plot to rip people off for money to me,* he thought as he continued on his journey. He looked over to his left and noticed the sign there:

NO PEACE NO GOD, KNOW GOD KNOW PEACE

He realized then that he was still driving alongside the same section of road by the cornfield. "What in the world is going on here? I drive by here all the time and just read a sign and that I have never noticed before. And has this cornfield always been so long?" He continued driving and came back to the entrance of the road that led to the cabin. In bold print just as it was when he saw it the first time was the second sign:

Let GOD heal your heart and give you peace.

The road that Mr. James was on seemed to go on forever; there was no end to it. He continued driving and all he saw were the two signs, the road to the cabin and the cornfield. "I couldn't have lost my mind. It couldn't have happened to me. I've been a deacon in my church for over 30 years." After driving for a while, the thought finally came to him: *The next time you get to the entrance of the road that leads toward the cabin, make a detour and follow the sign with the arrow that promises peace.* Soon he was back at the side road that led to the cabin in the middle of the cornfield and he turned. He could not understand why the road that had once led him all across town was now leading him nowhere. This new road was sure to lead him on a path that he had never traveled before. As he made his exit onto the road that pointed to peace, he saw it sitting as big and run-down as it has always been: that old cabin, right in the middle of the cornfield. There was something drawing him to it like a magnet with a strong force. Mr. James finally pulled up in front of the cabin and the car shut off instantly. *"I wonder what else could go wrong?"* He said to himself. *"I wonder if they can help me with some gas in that cabin? This has got to be the craziest Sunday morning that I have ever had. It all just don't make sense!"*

He slowly opened the car door, got out, and walked toward the door. Just as he went to knock the door swung wide open. "Hey James come right on in. I thought you weren't ever gonna make it. We've been here waiting on you all morning long." Billy Ray said with a big smile. Mr. James was in total shock. After all, how did this old country hick know him? He knew that they had never met. "Can I get you something to drink like some water or fresh squeezed orange juice?"

"Uhhhh, yeah, I think I will take the orange juice. And you wouldn't have a lil shot of gin to add with it would yah?" James asked.

"Uhhhh No!" Billy Ray responded. "Shut up, sit down and be quiet! I can hear and see all three of you." At those words Mr. James began to violently convulse and fell to the ground as if he had been thrown physically. From his place on the floor he watched as three heads popped up through the center of his chest and began to argue with each other.

"I told you that our time was up. Why in the world would the Beautiful one bring us before a preacher who has power over us? It's all your fault!" Each of the spirits bickered among themselves. The Spirits fully emerged and were now standing beside Mr. James' limp body.

"Hold your peace and go into the abyss! You have controlled this man for too long!" Billy Ray commanded. Each of the spirits had their own unique hideousness. One of them looked like a sea ape with no hair but a scaly body. This one seemed to be the one that was reprimanding the other two. The second one's face kept transforming from a peaceful angel into a grotesque gargoyle-like creature. It kept screaming out religious slurs mixed with hate-filled profanity. The last one looked like a fat blob; it had small rotted teeth and moved about in a sensual manner. "I command you to leave James and to never return. May the hand of the Lord be against you." At those words, the evil spirits began to huddle together and tremble with fear; they looked about the room in every direction, as if they were expecting something to happen. Suddenly a giant hand from heaven swept down with a fierce force of wind and slapped all the demons; immediately they were turned into dust and blew out the window with the wind.

Mr. James opened his eyes and he sat up. "Wow, what was that?" he asked as he shook his head to clear the fog.

"That was the hand of the Almighty. So how do you feel?" Billy Ray asked.

"I feel different and new." Mr. James answered; there was a new sincerity in his tear-stained eyes. From that day forward, James Roberson's life was forever changed and for the better. His experience led him to develop a program designed to help young women who worked as prostitutes and who had been mentally and physically abused as a result. And the transformation all begin in a cabin in the middle of a cornfield.

Chapter 23

Time for a Change

"This is operator 911; how can I help you sir?"

"Yeah, my wife just stabbed my girlfriend and it's bad, very bad."

"Where's your location sir?"

"My wife and I are heading out of town but you can find my girlfriend, Trudy, in Routery Park, parked over by the lake in Medulla."

"What is the color of the car, make and model?"

"Listen lady you sure do ask a lot of questions. All I can say is it's a red or burgundy Cadillac. And it is parked by the lake," the man said.

"Sir what is your name? Sir? Sir?" The phone was dead.

The ambulance blared down the streets heading toward Routery Park. Trudy sat slumped over the steering wheel of her parked car; she was holding in her insides because she had been stabbed twice. The blood was oozing out of her mouth as she coughed. *How did I ever get myself into a predicament like this?* She thought. She faded in and out as the sweat began to drip down her face. *Oh it hurts, it hurts. He told me that he wasn't married. I saw the ring but I didn't care. How could I have been so stupid? I just wanted to have the life that I thought wasn't possible for a black woman coming out of the projects. Now it looks like I'm going to die here in this car. Brenda, I'm so sorry. Momma is so sorry.* Trudy passed out as she continued to lose blood.

The lake front was quiet and peaceful and there was not a cloud in the sky. Jonathan had decided to take a walk and ended up at the lake. There was a slight wind. He had been in prayer earlier that day; he had not heard from Brenda all day and for some reason she had been heavy on his mind. Finally he stopped and asked the Lord why.

"Get to Lakeland Memorial Hospital right away," God responded.

"Should I contact Earl first?" Jonathan asked.

75

"No I have other work for him but right now. I just want you to go," God answered.

"What am I to do, and why am I going there?" Jonathan asked.

"Just trust Me and go my son and I will show you great and mighty things," said the Lord. Jonathan immediately took off toward the hospital which was 18 miles away. Although he did not have transportation, he no longer questioned God. He knew it was the plan of God to get to the hospital so the Lord would provide a way for him to get there.

Sure enough as he began to walk, a black 1975 Chevy Impala pulled up with a cloud of marijuana smoke coming out of the windows. "Hey mon, me see yah need a ride now boy?" the man asked.

"Well I thought I did but I think I'll be okay."

"Ah now don't be silly dere, now boy. It's only a little bit a weed smoke. It won't hurt yah that much mon."

The driver was a Jamaican straight from the islands. He had dreadlocks as wide as a lion's mane and as long as a yard stick. He wore a pair of dark sunglasses to hide his bloodshot eyes. There was a small bag of marijuana in the ashtray. He had a lit blunt in his hand and was holding it in his residue-burnt fingertips. *Lord, are you serious?* Jonathan asked in his mind. *Yes son; this is the ride that I have provided for you,* the Lord answered. *This looks like an impossible situation. Just look at this guy. This dude looks like a straight thug to me,* Jonathan thought. *He looks like the old version of Jonathan to Me,* the Lord reminded him. At that moment Jonathan's heart was smitten. *Lord, please forgive me for seeing the faults of this man and not seeing his need for You.* The Lord spoke back in Jonathan's heart, *All is forgiven My son.*

"So, what's your name?" Jonathan asked the driver.

"They call me Boogie Mon, but you can call me Boogie for short. I drive this way every day smoking a big spliff looking for someone to share it with but you don't like the type, eh?"

"No Boogie, I never touch the stuff anymore. I am a servant of a Man who does not hire the impaired to work for him." Jonathan replied.

"So who dis man you work for? Tell me and maybe he'll give me a job too." Boogie said.

"If he gave you a job would you do it well?"

"Listen mon, I am Jamaican; I do everything very well. What's wrong wit you, ask me this type a question?" Boogie asked forcefully.

"So you gonna tell me dis man's name or what?"

"Boogie, his name is Jesus." As soon as Jonathan got those words out of his mouth, the smoke cleared up from the marijuana and Jonathan proceeded to minister the words of life to Boogie under divine influence. Every word that Jonathan spoke was so full of the life and the power of God. He told Boogie that God loved him, had a plan for his life, and wanted to employ him in the heavenly kingdom. The whole atmosphere of the car began to change and there was what seemed like a cloud or a mist in the car. The thickness of the cloud got so strong until Boogie had to pull over to the side of the road because he could no longer drive under such influence. As Boogie listened to Jonathan's words he dropped his head and began to weep bitter tears of joy for his new-found relationship with Jesus. Slowly Boogie lifted his head to thank Jonathan for sharing such good news with him, but when he looked to the passenger seat, Jonathan was gone; it was if he had vanished into thin air. Boogie raised up both hands and glorified God for the wonderful things He had done.

The Spirit of God carried Jonathan away and he found himself at Lakeland Memorial Hospital. He looked up at the entrance sign in the room that he was standing in and noticed the sign next to it said "Emergency." At that moment the paramedics came rushing through the automatic sliding doors pushing a gurney. "We have to hurry up and get her to the back. She has lost a lot of blood. If we don't do something fast then we could lose her." One paramedic said to the other.

God spoke to Johnathan, "It's Trudy and she needs you to call upon Me so that I can answer your prayers on her behalf.

Brenda came rushing through the door. "I am looking for Mrs. Trudy Jackson," she said frantically to the receptionist at the front desk.

"She's been rushed back to I.C.U. and we can't allow you to go back right now," the receptionist said.

In her haste to get to the information desk, Brenda had not noticed Jonathan, who was pacing back and forth. He walked over to her and said, "It's gonna be all right. Let's just join our faith together in prayer." They both walked over to the emergency room chapel and found a place to kneel down at the foot of a wooden cross. Together, they began to pray.

"What in the world is going on with me?" Trudy thought as she felt herself moving rapidly downward through a wind tunnel. She saw the earth open up as if it was a mouth. She hovered over the top of the opening and each time it opened or closed, she felt a fierce heat ascend from what appeared to be a bottomless pit with flames and lava flowing through it. In the mist of the lava there appeared to be people being carried in a current that appeared to be a river of fire. There were murderous screams of pain coming up from the pit and Trudy had never heard anything like them before. All of a sudden a terrible presence appeared at the mouth-like opening in the earth and said, "Let her go. She's had her chance and now she belongs to me."

Trudy noticed that she was being held up by a pair of strong hands. She looked back to see a brightness that was the face of an angel. "No, I will not let her go. She is being held above this pit by the power of somebody's prayers. They are giving strength to my hands." Trudy's heart was beating faster and faster as she soon discovered that she was trapped in eternity and was facing the flames of the souls of people who lived their lives apart from Jesus.

She grabbed the angel, closed her eyes very tightly, and cried out to God. "Lord, give me just one more chance I'll do it much different, but please not my soul. Please not my soul!"

She then heard a voice like thunder. "Trudy, come back!" She saw herself ascending from the mouth of the pit at the speed of an eye blink. The pit vanished in the distance and soon she was moving backwards through the winding wind tunnel. As her spirit reentered the emergency room, she saw the doctors' frantically working on her body. With no resistance, she reentered her body. "Trudy, come back!" the Doctor said as the gauge on the respirator began to detect life once again. "Trudy, come back!" were the words she heard as she came to. As she lay there, she noticed all the tubes that were hooked up to her body that were pumping life-giving blood into her. "We almost didn't get this blood to you on time. You should be thankful for the new Jewish doctor on staff whose blood was a perfect match for you. If he had not banked a few gallons of his blood already, you would not have made it." She tried to look around to see this miracle doctor. "He stepped out of the room for a minute. He will be back to check on you and that's when you can thank him."

Trudy looked up and felt pain in her abdomen from the stab wounds. She managed to mumble out a few words, "What is his name so that I can thank him?" she asked weakly.

"I believe he said that he was Dr. Iesous Christos. I'll let you know for sure in a minute since it seems like he's taking a while to get back. A very strange thing, he says has been here for a long time. I guess it's just my first time seeing him. Nurse, could you do me a favor and check with the front desk and see if he is still in the building?" The handsome young doctor looked over to the nurse, who nodded in agreement and quickly headed out of the door. The doctor turned to follow but stopped to speak to Trudy again. "Oh yeah; you make sure you get some rest because you had a close call, young lady." Trudy lay there in bed with tears streaming down her face and thought about how she had been so determined to have such a good life here on earth, even at the expense of cheapening herself as a woman. *How blind was I?* She thought to herself. *Here I am, trying to build a life of luxury for myself at the expense of using men to get what I want. Little did I realize that my life could be snatched away at any moment, and I would find myself at the mouth of that horrible pit. What if that angel had dropped me?*

She shivered at what she imagined it would have been like. "Lord, I don't know much about you but it is true I believe that you exist. I've experienced you. I promise you that from this day forward I am willing to change my awful ways. Please give me the strength to keep this promise to you," she prayed.

The door of the chapel opened slowly as a doctor dressed in surgical shrubs, a mask, and gloves came in. "You two must be here for Mrs. Trudy Jackson," he said to Brenda and Jonathan.

"Yes, as a matter of fact we are." Jonathan answered.

"How is she, doctor?" asked Brenda.

"Oh she's fine. However it was a close call but I gave her some of my blood so that she can live."

"Thank you so much doctor. By the way sir, what is your name?" asked Jonathan.

"I am Dr. Iesous Christos. The fact is I heard your prayers down here in the chapel from upstairs. I decided that it would be good to come down and tell you that they worked," the Jewish doctor said. Brenda thanked God over and over for the life of her mother. Dr. Iesous looked at her. "You are very welcome." He almost added, "And God knows you're thankful" but he caught himself. "Now get on out of here and don't keep Trudy waiting," he said instead. Brenda and Jonathan grabbed each other by the hand rushed out the door. Before they could take two steps outside of the chapel. Brenda said to herself, *I forgot to thank him for the blood*. She turned around to go back into the chapel and he was gone.

She ran to catch up with Jonathan. "So did you thank him?" Jonathan asked.

She just smiled and said, "He knows I'm thankful."

As they got to the front desk, they could hear the surgical nurse talking with the receptionist. "Look again. I am sure that we have a Dr.

Iesous Christos in this hospital. He's the handsome Jewish guy who donated the blood for Mrs. Trudy Jackson."

"Listen honey, I don't know who gave you that blood but I can assure you that we don't have a doctor in this hospital with no ghetto name like that. The next thang you'll be telling me is to look up Nurse Sha Nae Nae," the heavy-set black receptionist joked as she sat behind the desk. "Now you and them doctors back there, y'all just need to get it together," she finished sarcastically and turned away from the nurse. With an abrupt "Next!" she called for the person standing in line.

The surgical nurse walked away, shaking her head in confusion. Jonathan and Brenda looked at each other, and at the same time looked up and said, "Thank you, Lord."

The blood that was now flowing through Trudy's veins was not only good for giving natural life but it also guaranteed that she would receive spiritual life; the English translation of Iesous Christos is Jesus Christ. His blood never loses its power to save lives or snatch souls from the very mouth of hell.

Jonathan and Brenda walked into the small hospital room. Trudy had her head propped up on a pillow. Brenda walked over and kissed her mother on the forehead. "Baby I am so sorry that you have to see me like this." Trudy struggled to speak.

"Shhh, Momma. It's okay." Brenda responded as tears streamed down her face. "You don't have to say a word, Momma. I am just happy that I still have my best friend right here with me. For a quick moment I thought that we lost you." Jonathan walked over and joined hands with the two ladies; he had Trudy repeat a prayer asking Jesus to come into her heart. Deep down inside, Trudy knew that she would never again visit that awful pit that she had encountered moments earlier. It seemed that everything in the room had changed. Trudy's new perspective let her see that everything was as beautiful as a ray of sun that shone through her window.

All three of them knew that God was pleased with what had just taken place in their midst. From that day forward, Trudy Jackson would never be the same. She would learn to live and love life all over again, just as if she had become an innocent child; she would learn to depend upon God as her source and not on the men who had been willing to be used by her just so that they could use her for her body.

Trudy's story is like so many others' stories. It depicts a truth of how people everywhere are reaching for temporary pleasure rather than finding the lasting joy that can only be found in God. Well Trudy found it and it all started with two young men in the cabin in the middle of the cornfield.

The alarm clock went off with an agitating sound. As Mildred rolled over to shut it off, a thought went through her hazy mind: it was Monday morning, which meant another long day at the diner. She slowly dragged herself out of the bed and grabbed the remote control for the T.V. She pushed the power button and headed into the bathroom that was connected to the master bedroom. *That must have been some good weed because I don't even remember going to bed last night*, she thought. In the other room, she could barely hear the morning news broadcast over her electric toothbrush. She hurried up and finished brushing her teeth.

"*Chaos erupted in the Ponce De Leon housing projects in Tampa last night,*" the anchor man was continuing a story as Mildred went back into the bedroom. "*And we have our very own Suzan Seals at the scene this morning to give us the update. Suzan?*"

"*Oh yes Pat! This is a terribly tragic situation that took place here last night. It all started when that black Mercedes Benz you see there in the background behind me pulled into the housing project. Neighbors say that a slender black male wearing a black hoody sports jacket rushed over to the car and fired into the vehicle until the gun clip was empty. At this point the local authorities have no leads on the shooter. However, we do have the identification of the victim. The victim is believed to be an area known drug dealer, known by the locals as Travon "Tookie" Thatcher.*"

The room went silent. Mildred could see the anchor person, but could hear no sound; she was in shock after hearing the devastating news. *Oh my God, no. Not Tookie! Not Tookie! Not my only brother! Not my only brother!* Ran through Mildred's mind over and over again.

More pain visiting the heart of another misguided life: How could anything good ever come out of this type of situation?

Mildred slumped to the floor as if her breath had been knocked out of her. She lay curled up in a corner of her bedroom, lifeless and limp; only the tears streaming down her face indicated life. She was all alone in the world: no mother, no father, and now her only beloved brother was gone. All gone. She slowly made her way to her feet and after making her way down the hallway, walked into the guest bedroom. She reached up on the shelf to retrieve a black shoebox from it. The box held the drugs that Tookie had left with her just two days earlier.

As she opened the box, she heard her brother's sweet and caring voice. She remembered him saying, "Now sis, hear me and hear me well. You don't want to get caught up with this stuff." She grabbed the lid and quickly placed it back on the box. She reached over by the bed stand and picked up the phone to call Kathy to tell her the horrible news about Tookie's death and to let her know that she would not be coming to work. She dialed the number and got Kathy's voicemail. *Hello. This is Kathy Franklyn. I am not in right now. If you would please leave your name and number, I will return your call as soon as possible. Thank you and have a blessed day. Beeeeeep!* "Hello Kathy; I need you to cover for me. Something terrible has happened to Tookie. Apparently, he was shot and killed last night. I am probably gonna have to go to Tampa and claim the body." She spoke with the stab of pain barely masked in her voice. "Give me a call when you get this message." She pulled herself through the most difficult voice message that she believed she ever had to make. She hung up the phone and for the first time in her life the thought of just giving up on life ran through her mind. She looked over once again at the black shoebox and her stomach began to turn over.

Three months later:

"Hey honey, would you like a date?" The old scruffy-looking man pulled up behind the frail woman who stood outside of the vacant building that used to be Mildred's Diner. The woman with the too-short skirt got into the man's Suburban. "Honey, you sure do look familiar to me," the man tried to start a conversation.

"No, you don't know me," the young woman strongly stated.

"No, but I just can't help feeling as if I know you."

"Listen man, time is money and from the moment I stepped into this truck you was forty dollars in my debt." The man overlooked her sarcasm and suddenly slammed on the breaks; if it had not been for the seatbelts, they would have hit their heads on the dash board.

"Man, what's wrong with you?" she hollered in anger.

The man reached over and pulled the pair of dark sunglasses from the woman's face. "Mildred Thatcher! I heard it, but I didn't believe it."

"Sir, you can just let me out of this truck because our business deal is off."

"Now honey, don't be like that," the old scruffy man continued. "Your secret is safe with me Mildred. I won't tell if you won't." Without a word, Mildred reached over, grabbed the door handle, quickly opened the door, and got out of the truck. "All of you no good for nothing tramp whores are the same. And just to think, you had one of the finest diners in this town. Now you are nothing but a good for nothing crack whore. You're nothing! Do you hear me? Absolutely nothing!" The man yelled out as he drove off.

"Tookie, look at me. Look at what I turned out to be." She said, talking to herself as she walked down the old familiar dirt road. "Who would have thought that after your death, bro that I would have come to this. At your funeral, it was so hard seeing you lying there in that box. There's nothing left for me to do but escape the pain through these drugs. Maybe life will be good to me and punch my ticket as well." She reached into her bra and retrieved the crack wrapped in a plastic baggy. "I am so sorry, Bro. Until that day comes, this the only escape that I know." She loaded the substance into her pipe, took a lighter and lit it, then went off into her own tormented euphoria. After she blew out the smoke of that drug, she felt as if she was in another world, a world where there were no human feelings. A world where she could see demons operating through the bodies and minds of other people. *You are going to die just like Tookie,* the many voices in the atmosphere told her. *Look at you, you dirty nasty street whore. You will never be nothing more than what you are. And then you will die like Tookie died.* The voices continued: *Everybody around you hates you because you are a loser and a crack head, a piece of dog feces.* The more the voices tormented her mind the more drugs she used to escape. It did not work because the voices only got louder.

Shawn R. Mosley

Chapter 24

The Other Realm Which is Unseen

The grotesque and hideous creatures hovered around Mildred every time she inhaled and blew out the smoke.

They were evil spirits under the direct orders of a ruling demon of witchcraft known as Hacate. This evil spirit controlled the underworld. Its primary purpose was to take the will of choice away from Mildred and bring her totally under its influence, making her a manifestation of demon power in the everyday affairs of the many others who were under the same slavery to drugs.

"First, we must redefine her. In her past, she was a high achiever. So, now I must send ten different spirits of worthlessness and low self-esteem to her. Your jobs are to talk into her ear with all negativity that will break down her self-worth," Hacate said to his ambiguous army. "Next I want the spirit of whoredoms to give her a sense of power and deceit. Men who have any identifying spirits in them will be drawn to her and will fall under the power of witchcraft as well. I will anoint her and use her for my purpose! She will destroy homes and break up marriages, make bastards out of children, cause young men as well as old to lose their lives through drugs, disease and even murder. Yes, we will alter her really well."

At these words Hacate began to laugh and every demonic soldier under his authority let out a screeching laugh as well. There was celebration in the corridors of the unseen realm of hell. "Then I will kill her," he said.

Shawn R. Mosley

Chapter 25

On This Side of Life

Mildred continued to walk, unsure if she would make it through the day. But she knew one thing for sure; she was running out of dope and she needed to catch a trick real quick before she started to stress for more.

She walked over to the local Shell Gas Station and asked the clerk at the front desk for a key to get into the bathroom. "Listen, you no customer here. You cannot use restroom here," the Arabian clerk said.

She reached down into her bra and pulled out one dollar. "Give me a pack of Trident gum in the blue pack" and she threw the dollar on the counter.

The clerk picked up the dollar, turned around, got the gum, and handed Mildred a key that was chained to a small lawn mower tire. "Try not to hold up the restroom this time. I remember you from two days ago. You stay in the restroom for two hours."

Mildred took the key and went into the disgustingly stinky bathroom. She stood in front of the mirror and noticed that her black eye shadow was running down her face. *I guess it must have run as a result of all of these tears that I have cried.* She thought, *Anyhow, I don't have no time for that. I only have a few minutes to freshen up before that stupid old camel jockey comes knocking on the door.* She turned the water on and began to splash it all over her face. She reached into her small handbag and grabbed a face towel and bar of soap that was wrapped in some aluminum foil. She took the soap and put it in the towel and placed it under the running water until the wash cloth was full of foam. She removed her clothes and began to wash and wash and wash. It almost seemed as if she was trying to remove a stain from her very soul. The mind battles she experienced were sometimes long and fierce, but there was still something deep down on the inside of Mildred that got a chance to speak and that held a small light of hope. *You will make it out of this alive and you will be a much better person because of it,* it would say. This voice was very still and small, and was full of kindness and love. When it spoke to Mildred, all the negative voices ceased for a time. She brushed her hair back into a bun, put back on her same old clothes and slowly peeped out into the parking lot. She grabbed the key and walked back into the gas station.

The man behind the counter looked over the top of his glasses.

"You know the next time I am gonna charge you a dressing room fee!"

"Yadah! Yadah! Yadah!" she responded as she handed him back the key. She turned and walked out the door back into the night.

The other realm which is unseen

Hacate moved very carefully through the underworld, carrying a bottle very cautiously. In the distance and darkness all around him, there were red glowing eyes and growling beasts who loved to hide in the dark so that they could not be seen for what they really were. This was special training that all the demons received from Lucifer himself. The plan was to always stay in hiding, especially from all humans; the goal was to make people believe that the devil and demons did not exist. That was how he got them to believe that evil is of them and not of him. Hacate however was not walking alone; he never walks alone. He has many specialists who walk with him since the world of witchcraft is so diverse. As he walked, he had Pharmakia with him. Pharmakia's job was to control the world through the mindset of the people through potions that could be drank, swallowed, or smoked; the potions all have magic powers over the person's will. The potions are commonly known as drugs and alcohol. "Hacate: today I was much honored to present to you that bottle with the will of Mildred in it," Pharmakia said to his commander-in-chief.

"How stupid are most church people. They are so busy trying to find fault in each other until they are blind to the fact that we trap the wills and desires of men until they have no will to even want to be free! There's nothing that can get this trapped will out of this bottle except one thing and I am hoping not to have any interference from that One like he did with Trudy Jackson. What took place with her still makes me want to cuss and use strong profanity." Hecate said out of a heart full of anger.

Chapter 26

Medulla-One Town and One People

The town of Medulla quickly became a very special place to live. It was a place where no one was left to struggle alone. People came together and shared the problems of their neighbors; they helped each other. People pulled together to keep drugs out of their town. The heart of every man, woman, and child was focused on helping someone else. However, Jonathan wasn't finished with his work. He soon married Brenda and they moved to another small town in the Midwest called Muskegon, Michigan. The burden on both Jonathan and Brenda's hearts always included reaching out to young people who were in trouble and plagued by the many vices that seem to trap and snare them.

It is amazing how God could use an old wooden cabin in the middle of a cornfield to transform the lives of people who then one day will change the world.

Shawn R. Mosley

Made in the USA
Charleston, SC
30 June 2014